Blin ~~ok her head.~~

This must not be Devlin. But it was. His all too familiar face with a firm mouth that used to tease her skin into believing it was alive with a fire of its own, the easy grace in his movements that spoke of knowledge and determination as he straightened up holding one end of the plinth, the confidence that exuded from every pore of his body. This man was none other than her ex-fiancé. Of all the people to turn up today when she was feeling relaxed and happy after a wonderful break. What had she done to upset the universe? There were plenty of doctors out there, though not necessarily available or good enough for the position here. So just because she didn't want Devlin Walsh to be the new specialist in the department didn't mean she could have it her own way. But hell, she could still scream at the sky about this. Silently, of course.

Dear Reader,

Can two passionate people reignite a relationship that imploded seven years earlier? Chloe and Devlin have no intention of ever getting together again after all the hurt they dealt each other, but when a couple is meant to be together no matter what, they are fighting a losing battle.

Working in the same emergency department means they have to get along for at least eight hours a day, and in no time at all, it isn't enough. Old feelings and love begin to surface and neither of them can fight it.

I hope you enjoy reading their story of how they overcome the past and fall in love all over again. Or had they never actually stopped loving each other?

I'd love to hear from you at suemackayauthor@gmail.com.

Sue MacKay

www.SueMacKay.co.nz

THEIR SECOND CHANCE IN ER

SUE MacKAY

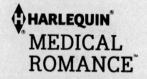

HARLEQUIN®
MEDICAL ROMANCE™

Recycling programs for this product may not exist in your area.

ISBN-13: 978-1-335-40921-8

Their Second Chance in ER

Copyright © 2022 by Sue MacKay

This edition published by arrangement with Harlequin Books S.A.

For questions and comments about the quality of this book, please contact us at CustomerService@Harlequin.com.

Harlequin Enterprises ULC
22 Adelaide St. West, 41st Floor
Toronto, Ontario M5H 4E3, Canada
www.Harlequin.com

Printed in U.S.A.

Sue MacKay lives with her husband in New Zealand's beautiful Marlborough Sounds, with the water on her doorstep and the birds and the trees at her back door. It is the perfect setting to indulge her passions of entertaining friends by cooking them sumptuous meals, drinking fabulous wine, going for hill walks or kayaking around the bay—and, of course, writing stories.

Books by Sue MacKay

Harlequin Medical Romance

Queenstown Search & Rescue

Captivated by Her Runaway Doc
A Single Dad to Rescue Her
From Best Friend to I Do?

London Hospital Midwives

A Fling to Steal Her Heart

Take a Chance on the Single Dad
The Nurse's Twin Surprise
Reclaiming Her Army Doc Husband
The Nurse's Secret
The GP's Secret Baby Wish

Visit the Author Profile page
at Harlequin.com for more titles.

This one is for all those special family and friends for their wonderful support over the past couple of weeks. It has meant the world to me. Love, Sue

CHAPTER ONE

'Wait till you meet the new doc,' Jaz told Chloe as she closed her locker. 'He started last week and has already got half the hospital talking about him.'

Laughing, Chloe headed out to the emergency department workstation. 'How many times have I heard this? Every male doctor who comes to work in the emergency department starts out as the best thing since mobile phones.' Not that she often disagreed, but she did keep her distance. In her experience some of them had egos that gave them expectations of how they should be treated as perfect while quick to find flaws within her.

'Even you might look twice this time.'

Jaz had no idea how often she'd looked at the previous emergency specialist until they'd learned he had a wife and two kids back in Christchurch whom he'd forgotten to mention to the women he'd dated here. Thankfully,

Chloe sighed, she'd only looked and turned down his suggestion of a night on the town together because something about him hadn't gelled.

'So who is this man? What shifts is he working this week?' Chloe was in zone three, the area for the most serious injuries and illnesses that presented, from seven to three all week. Being prepared for any changes was important to her. Especially new doctors as they nearly always had their own way of doing things—how they approached patients and what they expected from the nurses—and it was best to be prepared. Saved a load of hassle.

An orderly charged into the hub in the centre of the department, calling, 'Man down in Reception. Not breathing.'

'You're not in the army any more, Willy,' Chloe quipped as she snatched up a defibrillator from the trolley by the bench. 'Jaz, you hear that?'

'Right behind you,' her friend answered.

'Nothing like diving straight back into work,' Chloe muttered as she sped past the mostly empty patient cubicles and down the short corridor to Reception. A fortnight at her parents' home in the Marlborough Sounds using up some holidays she was owed and supposedly taking care of her mum post major abdominal surgery had been bliss. There'd been little to do since her mother was stubborn and didn't take kindly to lazing around recuperating. They'd had a couple of minor squabbles about what her mother should not be doing, all in good fun.

The time had been the perfect elixir for her own worn-out body and mind following hectic weeks working long hours with few days off because of a sudden shortage of nurses due to one giving birth ten weeks early, another suffering from a broken femur, and a third one dealing with a family crisis. Plus the doctor who'd had to quit in a hurry when her husband broke his back after falling off the roof of their house he was fixing had added to everyone's workload. As a senior nurse, Chloe was kept very busy, which mostly she liked. It had been a concern that she mightn't get her time off to go to the Sounds, but in the end it had all worked out fine. Seemed as though they were now fully up to speed on staff levels with the new doctor having started. Bring him on.

Willy thumbed the door-release button. 'I've got the door for you.'

Skidding to a stop by the sprawled body, Chloe placed the defib on the floor and dropped to her knees by the woman—not man, Willy—and immediately lifted her wrist to feel for a pulse.

Jaz appeared opposite her. 'Anything?'

'No.' Chloe tore open the woman's shirt, interlaced her fingers and began compressions on the chest. 'You take the defib.'

Jaz was already placing pads on the exposed chest. 'Anyone know the lady's name?'

'Wendy Wright,' gasped a man standing to the side, shock echoing through the room. 'My wife.'

'What happened?' Chloe asked, without looking up.

'She woke me at about five, said she'd been having sharp pains in her chest for about an hour. I wanted to call the ambulance but Wendy said no, I should bring her in. We only live five kilometres away.'

Five kilometres wasn't far, but an ambulance came fully equipped with lifesaving apparatus. Push, lift, push. Twenty-four, twenty-five. 'Jaz, you ready to administer two breaths?' Twenty-nine.

'Yes.'

Thirty. 'Go.' Chloe withdrew her hands, rolled her shoulders. 'Has your wife got any history of heart problems?' The woman looked fit and healthy, but looks could be deceiving.

'No. She goes to the gym four times a week, runs, eats healthy food, doesn't drink.'

The door heading into the department opened, then closed. Even when the air shifted around her with an oddly familiar sensation, Chloe remained focused on Wendy, and started more compressions. Why would anyone make her feel warm at a moment like this? It was daft. Her eyes didn't leave her patient as she tried to ignore the slight lifting of the skin on the backs of her hands.

'Family history of heart problems?' Jaz asked the husband while holding the defibrillator pads ready to place on the woman's chest the moment the machine's electric current was ready.

'None.'

Push, release, push. Sweat was already breaking out on Chloe's forehead. Doing compressions was no stroll in the park.

Jaz said clearly, 'Stay back, Chloe, everyone.'

Removing her hands and making sure she wasn't touching the woman anywhere, Chloe waited, rubbing her hands up and down her arms, eyes glued to the monitor as the current struck the heart. 'Nothing.' Hands together, press, release. 'One, two, three, four.' She continued while waiting for the defib's electric current to get up to speed again. The woman's face looked deathly pale. It would be horrifying for her husband to be watching this. *Come on, Wendy. You can do this. Your heart needs to pump all by itself. Come on.*

Jaz said, 'Stay back. Second shock coming up.'

The flat green line on the screen lifted, dropped, lifted, up and down, a rough line replicating erratic heartbeats showing life. 'Thank goodness.' Relief surged through Chloe as she tipped her head back to ease the tension in her neck and shoulders from doing the compressions. Then she shrugged forward and lifted the woman's wrist and felt the pulse just to be certain. *Yes.* The heart was sending blood around the body, taking oxygen to where it was most needed, keeping Wendy alive. A good result to be going on with. 'Willy, we need a bed in here. Plus a plinth to slide Wendy onto.' It made lifting a patient onto the bed easier on everyone's backs and saved further injury to the patient.

'Everything's ready and waiting on the other side of the door.' Willy was usually one step ahead of things, and rarely got it wrong about what was required.

'Good one. Bring it through.' Chloe staggered to her feet, pins and needles shooting through her calf muscles, and rubbed away the tension in her arms brought on with the compressions. It was always a worry they wouldn't get a heart restarted. She'd experienced that a few times in her career as an emergency nurse and the following despondency always took a bit of getting past, even when knowing it wasn't possible to save every person every time.

Within moments Wendy had been moved onto the plinth and Chloe was reaching for a corner to help lift it onto the bed.

'I'll take that end.'

Chloe froze, her hand inches from the plinth handle. Every muscle in her body was on high alert. Her eyes must've widened because the skin at the corners suddenly felt tight. That voice brought back so many memories she no longer had a use for. Or wanted to revisit. Not at all.

A tall, slight man reached down to take the end of the plinth, his hand missing hers by mere millimetres. Devlin Walsh. It couldn't be. But even if she hadn't recognised the voice, she knew that tiny tattoo of a star between the thumb and forefinger. No doubting who this man was. What was he doing? Ahh, got it. No wonder the air had shifted around her earlier. It had been trying to warn her of trouble. This was the new doctor. The good-looking one every female wanted to get their hands on. They were more than welcome to him.

Ladies, he knows how to break hearts without pausing for a breath. He doesn't understand the truth, even when it knocks him between the eyes. He sees life through rose-tinted, make that wealth-inspired, glasses.

'Chloe, out of the way,' Jaz said. 'We've got this.'

Blindly stepping back, she shook her head. This must not be Devlin. But it was. His all too familiar face with a firm mouth that used to tease her skin into believing it was alive with a fire of its own, the easy grace in his movements that spoke of knowledge and determination as he straightened up holding one end of the plinth, the confidence that exuded from every pore of his body. This man was none other than her ex-fiancé. Of all the people to turn up today when she was feeling relaxed and happy after a wonderful break. What had she done to upset the universe? There were plenty of doctors out there, though not necessarily available or good enough for the position here. So just because she didn't want Devlin Walsh to be the new specialist in the department, didn't mean she could have it her own way. But hell, she could still scream at the sky about this. Silently, of course.

The moisture in her mouth evaporated. After all this time she wouldn't find anything remotely exciting about Devlin. They'd been finished for almost seven years. She closed her eyes, then opened them again, but felt only annoyance. She'd lost the love of her heart and the baby she'd been carrying within a couple of weeks. Forget annoyance. It was pure anger hissing in her veins. He was real, and absolutely *not* exciting. Definitely the rat who broke her heart. Turned out when the going got tough she hadn't been good enough for his family, and therefore him. Growing up in the lowest of the low suburbs in Auckland, according to Mr and Mrs Walsh, she wasn't supposed to mix with the crème de la crème. An opinion that had never changed. Crème de la crème? More like super *rico*. So full of their own self-importance they didn't know if they were coming or going half the time. Bet they wouldn't believe she'd never missed them or their lifestyle one little bit. Not when they believed she'd got together with Devlin for his money, not because she loved him.

'Chloe, you want to grab the defib?' Jaz asked over her shoulder as the bed with their patient was pushed into the department.

The exaggerated wink Jaz gave suggested Chloe might be aware of Devlin in ways Jaz had said other women were, which reminded Chloe to get her head straight. It also made her stomach churn at the thought her friend could even imagine she'd be interested in the new doc. Not that Jaz knew much about her past, especially about Dr Walsh. He was old news. He'd never intrigue her with his wicked wit and sexy body again. Been there, fallen in love deep and fast, did the excruciating hard yards on the way out, and barely managed to survive.

But she had, and now wasn't the time to be recalling all the reasons she didn't care two hoots for him. Devlin was working in the same department as her and there was no point making the days longer than they already were. Besides, any conflict between them would just make everyone else uncomfortable around them, and hadn't she got over him? Yes, she had, so she'd act appropriately.

Putting the defibrillator back on the trolley, her hand briefly touching her churning belly lightly, she turned for the cubicle where they'd taken their patient. Reality dropped like a boulder. Devlin was here to stay. He wasn't an apparition. Unfortunately.

Welcome back, Chloe. Hope you had a great holiday because your job has just taken on a whole new dimension and it's not looking too great right now.

Deep breath. But it would improve. It had to. This time she wasn't going to be the one to leave. The experiences she'd had as part of moving on from her broken engagement had made her stronger and more resilient. Hadn't they? Guess that theory was going to be put to the test over the coming months.

Stepping up, she breathed deep, pulled on her professional face, and said, 'Hi there, Devlin. Welcome aboard.'

Devlin glanced up from their patient to Chloe Rasmussen, charging the air around him as she entered the cubicle where they'd brought Wendy. 'Hello, Chloe, and thank you. I'm slowly getting to know everyone,' he said from the other side of the bed, caution overtaking everything else as he looked at his ex-fiancée.

Unfortunately he knew her too well, so why the wave of illogical fascination crashing through him? So many years since they'd split up, and though he'd learned last week she worked in this department and would be here this morning, he'd had no qualms about that because of all those years standing between then and now. He hadn't been carrying a torch for her all that time. Not even a match. Far from it. At twenty-seven, his heart had been so invested in her that they were planning on getting married. Then he'd found out she was cheating on him just as his previous girlfriend had. Straight away he'd wrapped his love up tight, tossed it aside, and walked away. Not only from Chloe, but the dream of settling down one day and having a family. A man could only be cheated on so many times, and for him it had been twice too often. He would never again take a chance on love. Some time during the intervening years of study and training, qualifying as an emergency specialist, he had got over Chloe, as he had the first woman who'd messed with his heart. Well and truly over her.

So why the tingling heat under his ribs brought on by a simple glance?

Right now Chloe was completely focused on their patient—as he should be. Hell. He never lost focus on what was important. Which certainly was not this slight, cool, pretty woman he used to know very well. Or so he'd thought until she'd proved how wrong he could be for a second time.

She was saying, 'Wendy, I'm sorry but I have to lift your blouse to place the pads on your skin,' as she prepared to attach the ECG monitor so they'd have continuous readings and an immediate recognition of cardiac arrest should it occur again. It shouldn't, but there was no such thing as never when it came to medicine and their patients. The beeps would vary according to the heart rate so if the heart stopped they'd instantly be made aware by a sharp monotone.

Wendy blinked her eyes open, sought out her husband, and closed them again.

'Mr Wright, I'm Devlin. These nurses are Jaz and Chloe. Sorry we didn't get around to introducing ourselves earlier but it was a little tense.'

'I understand. My name's Ian.'

'Ian, which GP does Wendy go to? I need to fill in the details that would normally have been down at Reception,' explained Jaz.

Devlin tried to listen to that nurse as she questioned the husband further, and to stop noticing Chloe as she attached the monitor leads to their patient. Getting distracted couldn't happen unless another crisis occurred in the department, and even then it was a controlled distraction. So he wasn't about to let Chloe sidetrack him any more than she already had.

Wendy's heart attack seemed to have come out of the blue. There was little info to work with, so he threw in some questions of his own. 'No history of chest pain, sore back, aches in the left arm?'

'Not that I know of.'

'Family history?' Sometimes it paid to repeat questions. Especially as at the time of Jaz's first queries the man was in shock and watching his lifeless wife lying on the floor while everyone worked to resuscitate her.

'None. Is she going to be all right?'

'We have to establish the cause of why her heart failed so there'll be tests done,' Devlin told him while dodging the question. He didn't yet have the definite answers the man was looking for. 'Did Wendy have any childhood illnesses?' Rheumatic fever would be one that'd possibly explain today's event, but she looked fit with well-honed muscles so that seemed unlikely. Besides her husband had told them she was healthy.

'Nothing.'

Jaz was tapping on the portable screen, filling in details.

Devlin sighed. He'd taken over, which showed Chloe was getting to him. Damn her. She'd lost that power years ago. Or so he'd believed. No, of course she had. 'Sorry, Jaz. Carry on. I'm going to take some bloods and call the cardiology department.' A specialist was needed now, not later. Except it wasn't even seven in the morning and unless there'd already been a cardiac emergency during the night the chances of a cardiologist being in the hospital that early were unlikely. He'd have to get someone out of the shower or away from breakfast. He shrugged. It was the nature of the job. Though not his, unless there was a particularly hectic shift and more hands were required. Which did happen more times than he cared to acknowledge in emergency departments, especially on a Friday or Saturday night when downtown partying got out of control.

'Heart rate's thirty-four,' Chloe noted aloud.

Not good. 'Too low.' Did she still like to party? Dance with abandon to loud music? Shake her shapely backside and wriggle her hips until he'd had to have her? 'Monitor it,' he snapped.

Perfectly shaped dark eyebrows rose. 'Yes, Doctor, I am.'

Two mistakes in not many more seconds. He shook his head sharply. 'Sorry, Chloe. You know what you're doing. I get that.'

'I do.'

'You two obviously know each other,' Jaz commented, looking from one to the other of them with a question in her eye.

'It was a long time ago,' Chloe said.

Too well. Though not well enough when it came to the crunch. He might've once made the mistake of falling for Chloe and asking her to be his wife, but he'd learnt a blunt lesson when she played around on him. Don't trust women with his heart. But he could still be professional—kind and friendly, not overbearing and rude. Guilt ripped through him. He had been abrupt with Chloe for no reason other than his own musings over the past. 'I haven't seen Chloe since not long after she qualified as a nurse. She was focused back then, and I'm sure that hasn't changed.'

'I try to be.' Chloe spoke sharply while her eyes remained fixed on the monitor as she prepared a cannula to insert in Wendy's arm so they could give any intravenous drugs and painkillers she required over the coming hours. They'd also be getting fluids on board through another cannula as dehydration did not help in this situation. 'Devlin was studying to become an emergency specialist back then.'

So she wasn't completely denying their past. Was that good or bad? Warmth touched his skin. Kind of odd when she'd hurt him so badly. *Suck it in, get on with being professional.*

'You did well with the compressions today.' Now he sounded condescending. She really had got to him—without saying anything at all annoying. 'I mean it. I got there just behind you and Jaz, and wanted to leap in and take over, but you had it under control.' His instinct had been to push them aside to do the compressions himself. After all, he was the emergency specialist. Once he would've done exactly that, but nowadays his ego was a lot more secure and he stood back to let others perform their tasks just as competently as he could. He didn't have to prove himself any more. He was a very good

emergency specialist. Yet somehow Chloe had
made him feel superfluous.

Also in awe at the speed and proficiency
of both women working on their patient. His
palms had itched with the need to get in there
and save the woman sprawled on the floor, but
he'd forced himself to stay put. Everything
that could have been done for Wendy was already being done efficiently and effectively.
Interrupting would've only caused problems.
So instead, his gaze had turned to Chloe as
she'd continued her efforts. There had been no
panic or stress on her face, only concentration
as she'd done her job. As she was one of the
permanent nurses working any of the three typical shifts, they were going to rub shoulders a
lot. And he'd already snapped at her.

Great going, Dev.

Chloe might've always taken her career seriously, tried hard to overcome a lack of confidence in herself, but there'd been another, much
livelier side to her when they'd been together
away from work. She'd said she had years to
make up for of studying and working at su-
permarkets stacking shelves to pay her way.
She'd done a lot of that. Apparently he hadn't
been enough for her; she'd needed other men as
well to play catch-up with. She'd waited until
they were engaged, and then let rip, apparently

certain the ring on her finger meant she was safe from being dumped if the truth ever came out. Bile rose in his throat. He swallowed hard. She'd betrayed him, hurt him.

Old hat, Devlin. Get over yourself. Get over Chloe. Again.

'Want me to get the blood-test kit so I can do the tests?' Chloe asked, her face blank, her slim frame ramrod-straight and tense.

What? Damn, he was losing the plot. 'No. I'm on my way.' He forced himself to turn away and head for his desk in the centre of the department. Giving her the hug he found he inexplicably wanted to share after saving Wendy's life would be like wrapping his arms around an iceberg. She wouldn't be warm towards him after the way they'd parted. She'd been so furious when he'd left her, even though it was her own fault. Besides, to hug her at work would be bad enough. To hug her at all when she meant nothing to him any more would be just weird. No denying he wanted to though. She'd think he had lost his mind. She might have a point, he conceded as he sank onto the chair and picked up the phone to call the cardiology ward.

When indifference should be foremost in his head, that wasn't what was pricking his mind. His gaze wandered towards the cubicle where Chloe was talking to Wendy, reading the monitor, and looking more self-contained than he remembered her ever being. She'd constantly worried about not being good enough for him and his family, her lack of confidence made worse by his mother, who hadn't taken a shine to her future daughter-in-law. Then Chloe had had a brief fling with another man. Only brief because he'd quickly found out and told her they were over, though. None of it had made sense. He had adored her, had promised her the earth and had been looking forward to being married and having a family with her later on. She'd said she felt the same and he'd believed her.

Old words filtered into his head.

You and your family are all so wrapped up in your wealthy bubble that none of you see other people for who they truly are. Try standing in a different pair of shoes some time and see how the world looks from another perspective. I am as good as any of you.

He'd had no idea where that had come from, and used to shrug her doubts away, telling her she was more than good enough for him and that was all that mattered. Then she'd played around on him. If she'd felt she didn't fit in why go and do the very thing that proved his mother right about her? Did she ever have any regrets? Or had she moved on, found someone else to settle down with, and was now happy in a way he obviously hadn't made her? Chances were she had a husband, kids, and a mortgage like most normal people. Unlike him. After twice having his heart broken, he stuck to the tried and true habit of dating amazing women and then walking away before anyone got too involved. It worked for him, kept him safe, and at the end of the day he was okay with that.

'Cardiology. Don't tell me you've got another emergency down there,' came a disgruntled male voice over the phone. 'I've been here all night.'

Devlin smiled. 'Sure have. Devlin Walsh here. A forty-three-year-old woman had an arrest in the waiting room—' he glanced at his watch '—twenty minutes ago. She's been resuscitated. No history of heart problems, appears fit and healthy.'

'This is Nick Somers. I haven't met you yet, but seems I'm about to. I'll be down shortly.' No mucking about.

Devlin liked that. 'Thanks.' Hanging up, he filled in a lab form on screen before going to get the blood kit. 'Nick's on his way down from Cardiology,' he told Chloe and Jaz when he returned to the cubicle. 'Seems they've had a busy night.'

Chloe glanced his way. 'I haven't had time

to catch up with who's in here, let alone what went down during the night. I'd hardly stepped into the department and Willy was calling for help with Wendy.'

'Much the same for me,' Devlin admitted, relieved she was talking to him as she might any doctor. That stiffness in her shoulders had loosened and there was even something approaching a smile in those oval caramel eyes. It made sense she might've been a little shocked when she first saw him, since she'd been on leave and probably wouldn't have had a clue he now worked here. 'I'd better get onto finding out what other cases we have.'

'What bloods do you want done for Wendy?' She was holding her hand out for the kit.

'A troponin to see what level it's at and set the bar for further tests, plus general liver and renal tests and a CBC. Cover the bases and if Nick wants to add any more we'll have taken the correct samples.'

'Right. I'll do that.'

It was the second time she'd mentioned she'd take the bloods. Was he lagging behind that much? When he looked directly at her, his heart lurched. Those eyes used to be full of happiness whenever she was with him. Even love. Until the day he'd walked into her flat and accused her of sleeping with another man. A tsunami of pain had replaced the happiness then, pain he'd thought she deserved. Today only professionalism showed. Fair enough. That was how he wanted it to be, despite the unexpected memories of what had once been the most wonderful time of his life. He'd never trust her again so why consider if what he'd lost could be found? Even if at all possible, he wasn't running with it. She'd cheated on him.

She denied that, Dev.

Sure she did. So did his first serious girlfriend and he'd actually caught *her* in the act.

'You want me to do something else?' Chloe asked, sudden barbs in her voice at his lack of response.

'No.'

'Morning, everyone. Chloe, thank goodness you're back. The place isn't the same without your steady hand at the helm.' A short, chubby man strolled into the cubicle and held his hand out to Devlin. 'Nick Somers.'

'Devlin Walsh.' He shook hands, and then dipped his head in Wendy's direction. 'This is our patient, Wendy Wright, and her husband, Ian, behind you.'

'Hello, Wendy. I'm a cardiologist and will work with you to find out why your heart stopped.' He turned slightly and held out his hand again. 'Morning, Ian. Quite the stressful start to your day, I understand.'

'It certainly is. Glad to meet you.' Then he glanced at Devlin. 'Not that the doctor doesn't know what he's doing. And the nurses.'

Devlin said, 'Relax, Ian. I understand you want the best help on your side right now, and who better than a cardiologist?' Though he, Chloe and Jaz had done everything they could and needed to, and Wendy was all the better for that. Especially after the nurses had brought her back to life. Nick's job would be focused on finding the cause of the arrest and seeing that another didn't occur.

Chloe placed the blood-test kit on the bed. 'Wendy, there'll be a small prick.' She'd taken over the job he still hadn't got around to doing.

He sucked in his stomach, breathed deep to dissipate the frustration she invoked, and turned to Nick. 'I'll fill you in on the little we know.' And put all things Chloe, except her nursing skills, behind him. Again.

CHAPTER TWO

WHILE SIPPING HER TEA, Chloe stared at her running shoes. The morning had been busier than usual for a Monday so getting a break had come later and she was in need of a large caffeine fix. 'Nothing like a heart attack and a car accident to remind me that my real life is in here and not lounging on the deck overlooking the waters of the Kenepuru Sound.'

'Not to mention a hot doc that has everyone sitting up and taking notice,' Jaz added before biting into her muffin and looking smug.

'Not me.' Not in the way Jaz was suggesting. 'Don't even ask.' She'd once loved Devlin with every bone of her body and then some, and she'd thought she'd never get over him. But she had. Thank goodness or she'd be shattering into fragments right now. It had taken determination and hard work to move on, but she'd done it.

As she had her first love, Stephen, whom

she'd met at nineteen. She'd moved in with him at twenty, only to find enough courage to pack her bags and leave a year later when his controlling personality had become too much to bear. She hadn't ever been up to scratch for his exacting standards; something he'd loved to taunt her about, saying how useless she was at the basic things in life, and even worse in bed. Her leaving had shocked him, and he'd swiftly returned to being the nice guy she'd first met, begging for a second chance because he wanted to show how much he cared for her. She'd been stupid enough to believe him, but it hadn't taken long for Stephen to return to his old tricks, and it was easier leaving the second time, and staying away. She'd watched her mother do the same with a man who wouldn't accept Chloe as part of the package, and treated her worse than his cat, which was downtrodden and half starved.

Her mum had adored the guy, but no one, nothing, was allowed to hurt her daughter. It was a lesson that had taught Chloe to try to be strong and not let others wield the rod, no matter how much it hurt to walk away. She hadn't done very well at that. It had been hard when she'd believed Stephen was right in that she wasn't good at most things she did. Of course, she hadn't been strong, had argued with herself about what she was doing for weeks, but she had finally managed to leave.

But breaking up with Devlin had been a whole different story. He had never treated her badly, appeared to love her as much as she did him, until that fatal day when he'd arrived at her flat, taken one look at Adam in his semi-naked state, and accused her of having a fling behind his back. *Worse*, he'd refused to believe her explanation. Plain out refused to talk to her at all. Just walked away, head high, taking her heart with him. Yeah, it had been hard to get over that, but she had.

When she met Devlin two years after leaving Stephen while on placement on a plastic surgery ward during her final year of nursing training, she fell for him hard and fast. Seemed that was how it worked for her. But Dev had been just as quick to fall for her; they'd clicked with only a look, and seemed to be on the same page over many things—except his family. But she'd loved him so much she'd tried hard to fit into his privileged lifestyle, to make his parents accept her, especially after she and Devlin became engaged. It wasn't to be. Devlin threw her love back in her face hard and fast, decimating her with his complete lack of trust in her. He didn't even ask if it was true or try to discuss it with her. She was guilty in his eyes, and that was that.

Except she wasn't guilty. That he could so easily believe such a horrible thing about her had her doubting she'd ever trust herself to fall in love again. Her mother told her not to give up, to keep an open mind, when it came to men. There were some good ones out there, the only problem being they were hard to find. Her mother was forty-four when she finally met Jack, who loved her and treated her as though she was special, and was the closest to a real father Chloe had ever known. She was his 'little' princess, even now she was thirty-two years old.

So maybe one day she'd get lucky and find a man who'd believe in her and see her for who she was. A man who didn't complain about how she washed the dishes or made the bed, like Stephen. Or a man who didn't accuse her of something she'd never do, like Devlin. He'd also come with a snobbish mother who'd said things like, 'We're going to a charity dinner, not a pub meal,' as she'd studied Chloe's outfit. Or, 'The Hugheses are coming for drinks, not one of your nursing friends,' because Chloe hadn't gone to the hairdresser that day. She was one hell of a lot stronger these days, and a match for anyone. Her hands smoothed her uniform trousers over her thighs.

Jaz's voice cut through the mixed memories. 'Devlin's got your attention like no other guy I've seen you look at. You're miles away.'

Not that far, Chloe reflected. 'Not in the way you're thinking. It was a bit of a shock seeing him again,' she admitted. 'I can't get my head around the fact that there are doctors out there wanting to work here and it's Devlin Walsh who got the position. Couldn't they have found someone else?'

'You know the board's been interviewing prospects for a while now. He's definitely got what's needed here. We've been short-staffed since Kate's husband had his accident, and, despite what you say, good doctors weren't exactly lining up to replace her. There's a level of uncertainty about what'll happen when Lloyd's back on his feet and Kate considers returning to work.' Jaz gave her a broad smile.

'Even then, she'll probably only work part time,' Chloe acknowledged.

'So you're going to have to swallow that lemon in your throat and get used to working alongside Devlin.'

'I know.' Chloe shuddered.

It wasn't a lemon, but a strange feeling that the past was coming back in spades to haunt her. Maybe even knock her down after she'd worked so hard to get up and keep moving. She had loved Devlin so much, it was scary. What if some of that love was still lurking in her heart? Ready to cause pain every time she looked at him? Going to tip her steady world upside down again? As if. She gave a mental snort. He didn't belong in her heart any more. And she was stronger nowadays. *Remember?* First though, she had to get used to working with him.

'I understand how fortunate we are. He does have a brilliant reputation as an emergency doctor.' He always did, even when training. There was something about his calm, knowledgeable demeanour that repeatedly won patients and other doctors over. Plus his dedication. He'd won *her* heart. Too easily, perhaps. Because he was wonderful. Until… Until he threw her heart back in her face. No such dedication then. He couldn't have walked away any quicker.

His disabling words rose in her head.

'You've played around behind my back.'

'No, Devlin, I haven't. I never would.'

'Then explain why that man is in your lounge dressed only in a towel.'

'He needed a shower and has no hot water. I'm just being neighbourly.'

'Do you take me for a complete fool? Well, guess what? I'm not. I will not be made to look like an idiot. We're done, Chloe. It's as simple as that.'

There'd been nothing simple about watching Devlin walk out of her flat for the last time that night. Straightforward, maybe, but simple? Hell, no. Not when her heart was in a million little pieces. Not when he wouldn't talk to her from then on, no matter how often she'd tried to make contact. Not when her world had just stopped turning.

'So how long have you been working here, Chloe?'

Tea splashed onto her thigh, soaked through her blue uniform pants. How long had Devlin been standing behind her? Surely Jaz would've noticed and said something. He'd better not have overheard them talking. She didn't need Devlin knowing Jaz had told her to get a grip, or he'd realise he could still get her in a pickle. But he probably had already, all by himself. He had a gift when it came to reading people, especially her. Except for that one, disastrous time. 'About three years. I was at one of the private surgical hospitals here in Wellington before that.'

He'd crossed to the bench and was making

a mug of tea. 'You've been in Wellington all the time, then?'

Since you kicked me out of your life, you mean?

'No. I stayed on at the North Shore for nearly a year.' Wasting time hoping he'd see he'd made a huge mistake and come back to her. She'd have given him a second chance then, but that was before she'd learned to prioritise herself and her own needs. 'After that I took a break and headed offshore for a year. Next stop Wellington, and I'm settled, unlikely to leave.'

'Where did you go overseas?' He'd probably remember she never used to have any ambition to travel abroad.

She hadn't, even when boarding the flight to London on the way to Rome. It had taken coercion from her stepdad to get her packing a case with a year's clothing. 'Italy.' And only Italy. That'd surprise him even more because that length of time obviously meant it hadn't been a tour where everything was organised for her.

Sure enough, a teaspoon clattered into the sink. 'Italy? Did you work there?' He was studying her with something like amazement on his face. 'No, of course not. For one, you don't speak the language.'

'No, I couldn't work as a nurse. I boarded with a family in a small village near Milan and for my meals I taught their children English. I also took care of Nonna Rossi part time, and when I wasn't doing those things I went sightseeing, cycling everywhere. It was the most incredible experience of my life.' She'd never known such freedom, even while scraping by on very little—which hadn't been anything new for her anyway. With a roof over her head, a warm bed and food provided, and a wonderful family happy to share what they had, she hadn't needed anything more.

He winced. 'That's not something I'd thought you wanted to do.'

You didn't know me as well as you thought. Not enough to trust me anyway.

'It hadn't been.' But a lot of things had shifted in her thinking back then. The miscarriage she'd suffered not long after Devlin had left her had been a huge shock, especially as she hadn't even known she was pregnant. It had woken her up to realising she'd lost more than just a fiancé. She'd wanted to move beyond her dreams of love and children, since it obviously wasn't happening, and to find something to excite herself and give her confidence in her own ability to survive, and survive well. But she hadn't known how. It had been her stepdad, Jack, who'd got her up and running, not away from everything but heading towards something that could help her learn to be strong on her own.

'I'm impressed.'

Yeah, right. 'Don't be. I finally did something for myself.' That trip and the family who'd become such a part of her had widened her horizons so that she'd understood trying to make people love her, because her father had proved he didn't by not even waiting around for her to be born, wasn't as important as loving herself—and those like her mother and Jack, who always backed her. This was a side to her that hadn't been so obvious when Devlin was in her life.

'Sounds grand.'

There'd been nothing grand about her travels. She'd had a narrow bed in a back room in a small, dark and damp house with a family who ate lots of pasta and vegetables because they couldn't afford meat, and shared what little they had with her. And she'd loved every moment of it. Draining her tea, she stood up. 'I'd better get back.' It was barely ten minutes since she'd left the department.

Chloe put her mug in the dishwasher, reached for Jaz's and placed it in there too. 'Don't rush,' she told her friend as she headed for the door, needing Devlin-free air to breathe normally. Damn it. *Did* she still feel something for him after all this time? No, that would be too stupid. She wasn't the same woman who'd fallen for him. She no longer felt inadequate around strong, confident, privileged people. She'd learned to be herself, and accept that not everyone would see things her way. Her time in Italy had given her confidence and strength, and an inner comfort that had seen her come home and buy her little house and get a dog and live how *she* liked. Amongst that she'd learned not to look back and regret the past—except her miscarriage. Fingers crossed, one day she'd have another baby. Yet here she was, already getting in a bind over Devlin when there could never be a future between them. They'd hurt each other badly at the end. Not that she had been unfaithful to him, but he'd believed she had, so understandably he'd been hurt, too.

Jaz grinned. 'I'm coming. Wonder what we've got.'

Devlin told them, 'A three-year-old girl with a severe asthmatic episode. Mum's beside herself with fear. Clare's seeing to her.'

Chloe paused, turned back as her heart squeezed. 'The poor kid. She'll be terrified, especially if her mother's showing her fear.'

'You're right.' Dev nodded. 'They're both stressed to the max, and there's nothing anyone can do until wee Lilly's breathing properly again.'

Of course, he understood his patients' concerns. That was one of his best characteristics as a doctor. Actually, he'd been like that with her, too, about most worries she'd had. Tenderness threaded through her tight muscles, loosening the tension Devlin had brought with him. 'Where's the father?'

'He's on his way from the airport where he works. I hope he's the calm one of the family.'

'Me, too.' An easy smile started lifting her lips. Huh? Tightening her mouth, Chloe headed away.

'I'll work with Clare on this case,' Jaz said.

'Thanks, friend.' Not. She did not want to work with Devlin at all.

Swallowing the last of his tea, Devlin resisted the urge to get up and follow Chloe. Never in a million years would he have believed he'd feel anything but annoyance at spending time with her. He'd expected to be cool and calm, not sitting with his fingers gripping his mug while the blood pounded through his veins at a higher than normal rate. She looked lovelier than ever; time and experience had matured her. She'd lived in Italy for a year! Gone over on her own and stayed with a family in a village off the regular tourist track and begun to learn another language. That was not the Chloe he'd been engaged to. That Chloe hadn't been overly confident, always worried she wasn't good enough for people to stand by her. Her mother, Joy, had supported her but, from what he'd gathered, Chloe's father had never been in the picture and she felt guilty about the relationships Joy ditched when the men didn't want her daughter. Obviously she'd learnt to stand alone, since she'd moved here, where she didn't know other people. At least, she hadn't when he knew her, but any of the nurses she'd trained with might've moved south. Or maybe she now had a partner who came from here? He still had no idea if she was single or not.

Hell, when he'd dragged himself out of bed that morning after a restless night, unsure how it would go catching up with Chloe for the first time since they'd split up, he couldn't have cared less about her relationship status, yet within a few hours he'd twice wondered if there was a deep and meaningful other half in her life. Apparently Chloe still had the ability to get under his skin. So what? He'd cope. It wasn't a big deal. Some might say it was to be expected, given their fiery bust up. Not that he had anything he wanted to say to her about that. It was over, had been for years. In that time he'd moved on, qualified as a specialist, bought a house in Auckland, an apartment in Wellington, and become godfather to two of his friends' sons. His dreams of having a family with Chloe were long gone, and these days he made the most of time spent with his godsons while trying not to think about what he was missing out on.

He'd packed up and moved to a different city and a new job, and hopefully an exciting new life. All because his over-demanding parents had become even more so, lately. His brother, Patrick, had shown him by example that he could lead his own life. Patrick had disgraced the family by becoming addicted to gambling and had been told to go away until he was over his problems or he'd be cut off from the family wealth. So his brother had gone to Melbourne, got a high-end job in the financial district, quit gambling, and slowly found happiness. A new life, new friends, and a wonderful woman was all it took, he'd told Devlin. He had no intentions of returning home, which had left Devlin handling more of the family responsibilities. 'You should try it,' Patrick had added. 'You might be surprised what you find out about yourself.'

He had taken Patrick's words on board on a day when he'd put in far too many extra hours in the emergency department, where he'd lost a patient to cardiac arrest and worked hard to save a five-year-old from bleeding out after falling from a jungle-gym bar onto a glass bottle, only for their mother to start in on him about the daughter of close friends being the ideal woman to marry when he'd called in afterwards. That had been the final straw. He'd finally decided to get away and try something different. His parents were adamant he should marry that woman. She came from a similar background to his: the best schools, clothes and cars, trips to exclusive resorts around the world, high expectations over what they were to accomplish with their careers, which had to be respectable. A woman Devlin liked, but did not fancy. She was warm and funny, and devoted to her family, but that didn't add up to enough for him to think about marrying her and living with her for the rest of their lives.

Chloe. He'd been going to marry her, have children with her, be with her for ever. She'd touched him in ways he hadn't known before—or since. It was as though she could see right inside him to his vulnerabilities without using them against him. She'd given him a sense of belonging that came with no obligations.

'Devlin, we've got a stabbing victim.' Chloe, the nurse, not the woman taking up his head space, stood in the doorway, an ambulance patient form in her hand.

'Fill me in,' he demanded, following her to a cubicle where deep, teeth-gritting groans of pain were coming from.

'Tommy Drysdale, twenty-eight. Knife wounds to the chest and upper left arm, and at least one to the abdomen. No major blood vessels damaged. Patient had to be sedated as he was angry and tried to hit the paramedics who collected him. He's also been given morphine and is on fluids.'

'Has he taken any drugs? Alcohol?' That was when fighting often occurred: even before eleven in the morning with some people, which was obviously the case here.

'None that he's admitting to, but the paramedics noted the smell of alcohol on his breath, and his speech is slurred, which could also be due to his injuries or lack of hydration,' Chloe concluded.

'True.' No doubt a mix of all of the above. 'Hello, Tommy. I'm Devlin Walsh, a doctor. This is Chloe, one of our nurses.' The twitch of concern he suddenly felt for the staff made him speak carefully. The guy mightn't be in good shape right now, but Tommy looked like trouble. 'Tell me where the worst of the pain is.'

'Everywhere. It's twelve out of ten, man. Do

something about it instead of standing around talking at me.'

'How long ago was the morphine administered?' Devlin asked Chloe.

She read the form, checked her watch. 'Forty minutes. One milligram.'

'Can you please get another similar dose?'

'Sure.'

'Get me some water,' Tommy shouted. 'My mouth's dry.'

'Sorry but you can't have anything to drink or eat, at the moment.' Devlin lifted the swab applied to what appeared to be the largest wound near the right side of the horrid man's ribcage and pressed around the area. 'Any pain here?'

'Which part of everywhere don't you get?'

'I understand, but it will be worse in different places and I'm trying to find where so I know what internal damage has been done. Did you see how long the knife blade was?'

''Bout five inches.'

Dev winced, swallowed. The thought of something like that piercing his body made him shiver. He continued to check all the wounds. Whenever Tommy grunted at the pressure he applied he knew he'd found internal damage. Finally he straightened. 'I'm ordering an ultrasound of your abdomen and liver. I suspect your liver has been injured.'

Chloe held up the vial of morphine for him to check the batch number with her.

As she was pressing the drug in through the cannula, he told her, 'I'll stitch the lesser wounds. Can you call an orderly? Tell them it's urgent.'

She nodded. 'What about a moist pad for Tommy to suck since he can't swallow anything?'

'Yes, that's fine.' He walked out of the cubicle towards the cabinet containing suture needles and thread, said quietly, 'Tread carefully around him. I don't like the aggression in his eyes. I don't want anyone getting hurt.' *Especially not you.* There he went again. Thinking about Chloe more than other nurses. 'Warn anyone who might go into his cubicle to be aware.'

Her smile was grim. 'Believe me, I will. I've taken a hit before, and I don't intend letting it happen to me or anyone else again.'

His hands tightened. 'Someone hit you?'

'I took it on my shoulder. The shock of it rattled me more than the pain. It was a lesson I won't forget.'

'Good. But I don't like hearing that you were hit. I've taken a couple of knocks, and they made my blood boil. We try to help people and some of them show no appreciation whatsoever.'

'Dev, this sounds like a hobby horse of yours.' The skin at the edges of her eyes crinkled, but her mouth was tight. 'Drop it for now. You've got some suturing to do.'

All the air went out of him. She was right. He was not proving himself to be efficient or professional—to Chloe of all people. But he liked how she pointed it out without making a fuss or raising her voice. He would follow her example and maybe they'd manage to work together without any hassles about the past. Except it sat between them like a boulder that'd have to be manoeuvred out of the way with difficulty. 'On to it.' If only he could forget the Chloe who used to make his blood sing and his heart dance. He'd forgotten that about her until now, remembered only the immense disappointment and hurt that she could betray him when she'd sworn she loved him more than anyone or anything. That had been until this morning and seeing her for the first time in nearly seven years. The better memories were fast becoming a plague, filling every space in his head, which had to be why he was overreacting. Surely it would blow over fast? He only had to remember that man in her flat for that to happen. Didn't he?

'I doubt that blade was five inches long or there'd be more serious damage, wouldn't there?' she murmured.

'Hard to say. Depends if the assailant pushed it in right up to the hilt. With aggressive stabbing, they tend to pull out fast and have another go.'

She shuddered. 'Yuck. Gives me the creeps thinking about it.'

He touched her shoulder lightly. 'Me, too.'

The stunned look crossing her face made him withdraw instantly.

Quite right, Chloe. I shouldn't have touched you. I don't have the right to touch any of the staff. I never do that.

Yet he'd just placed his hand on her. Couldn't be because he wanted to get to know her again. That'd just be setting himself up for more pain. 'I'm sorry. I briefly forgot where I was.' Not who he was with though. Their conversation had felt personal, despite talking about something that all the staff in the ED had to deal with from time to time. When she'd shivered he'd felt the same urge to hug her that had caught him out earlier in Reception.

Chloe stepped away, picked up a phone from the desk and punched a number. 'Hi, it's Chloe in ED. We need an orderly urgently to take a man for an ultrasound. If Willy's available, that'd be great. The patient's aggressive.'

Devlin picked up another phone and rang through to Radiology. 'It's Devlin Walsh in ED. Sorry to do this to you, but I've got a man needing an urgent ultrasound of the abdomen. He's got stab wounds and I need to know if any organs have been damaged.'

'No problem. The machine's in use, but should be available in ten. The next patient will have to wait, that's all.'

Nothing unusual in that. 'Thanks.' Putting the phone down, he told Chloe, 'He's next in line.'

'Willy's on his way,' she told him. 'He's ex-army and takes no nonsense.'

He wanted to high-five her. She'd been onto the problem immediately. Instead he clenched his hands and said, 'The stitching will have to wait until Tommy gets back. The bleeding from all the wounds is mostly under control anyway. I think he's got off lightly.'

'I'll leave you to tell him that.' The tension had backed out of her stance. There was even a glimmer of a smile as she sat down at the computer to update a file. Though probably not for him.

'Think I'll keep it to myself for now.' What

a day this was. Not patient-wise, but when it came to behaving normally around Chloe he wasn't able to manage it. But then, she'd always been able to wind him up and have him wanting her with no effort on her part. Wanting her? He hadn't got that far. Nor was he going to any time in the future. If she could hurt him once, she could do it again. Damn it, why was he even thinking this? He'd got over her a long time ago. The anger and hurt had gone and he was a different person these days. He couldn't be sucked back into believing that when he loved someone he was actually loved back equally. Couldn't? Or wouldn't? Didn't matter, either way he wasn't getting involved with Chloe or any other woman.

His gaze fell on Chloe. That would be a shame. She was… She was still Chloe. Different, wonderful, exciting, sexy, loving. Except…

Give it a break, Dev. Go do some work.

He tossed a file into the tray on the desk and said, 'Anyone ready for a break while we still can?'

Jaz said, 'Chloe, you go first. I want to keep an eye on my patient for a bit longer.'

A scowl was directed at her as Chloe answered unenthusiastically, 'All right.'

A tea break, not a round on the wrestling mat, Devlin wanted to tease. Instead he walked beside her, quiet except for the thudding in his chest. This awkward situation could only get worse unless they dealt with it, and the sooner the better. 'Chloe. I understand you got a shock seeing me on your turf this morning.'

She didn't look his way. 'A little one but I'm over it already.'

'Then you're happy I'm here and we can get on with everything as though nothing even happened between us?' Tension was creeping into his arms and shoulders.

'Of course not.' She strode out, heading to the cafeteria at the end of the corridor. Suddenly she stopped, spun back to face him, hands tight at her sides, her eyes blazing. 'You could quit, go back to where you came from.'

If only. 'I won't do that. I'm sorry, but I'm here for the long haul.'

Her lips pressed into each other as she glared at him. She looked away, then back again. 'Okay, there are issues between us that were never resolved, and are never likely to be. In fact, they don't need to be. They're old and irrelevant now. I accept you're working here and that we have to get along for the sake of the rest of the staff and the patients. I can do this.'

'So can I. But I'd prefer that we are comfortable around each other, not uptight and wary.' Was it even possible? Probably after a month or two dodging around one another and not looking each other in the eye.

The slight flick of her tongue at the corner of her mouth told him Chloe had similar thoughts. 'You think we can manage that?'

'Only one way to find out.' He'd do his damnedest to make sure they did. 'I don't want to go on reliving what happened every time we cross paths. It's not me, nor is it like you, Chloe.' Her name skipped across his tongue and landed gently between them.

For a moment she said nothing, then finally a glimmer of a smile crossed her mouth. 'You're right. I hate carrying grudges, and this one is long dead anyway. As of now, we get along fine without becoming too friendly or talking about our previous lives in front of everyone.'

Exactly what he'd hoped for, yet the moment she said the words his gut dropped. He didn't belong in her life, nor she in his. That was going to be hard to live with. Because he couldn't write off all that they'd had together. Not now he'd come face to face with her again. Every look brought back some memory of wonderful times and why he'd fallen for her so hard in the first place.

He headed for the cafeteria. 'Coffee or tea?'

CHAPTER THREE

'Hi, Mum, how's your day been?'

Mine's been a shocker.

Chloe held her phone to her ear and watched her mutt, Genie, chase a seagull along the beach.

Make that disturbing.

Her reactions to Devlin were completely wrong. She was mad at him for coming to work in the same hospital as she did. Forget that he didn't have a clue she was there before he'd taken the job. And she was angry at the way he still affected her just looking at him. She'd thought that was long over.

'I played cards badly.' Her mother laughed. Her mum was still under don't-do-anything-strenuous orders from the surgeon.

'At least you weren't on the golf course.'

'As if Jack'd let me even look at my clubs. How was your first day back at work?'

Chloe looked out over the harbour from

where she stood on the heavy, damp sand at its lapping edge. With the familiar city centre and wharves to her left and a plane taking off from the airport to her right, the first sense of calm all day crept over her. 'Nothing like I expected. You'll never guess who joined the department while I was away.'

'Not Prince Charming, if the sound of your voice is anything to go by.'

Far from it. 'Devlin Walsh.' No further explanation needed. Her mum knew how badly he'd hurt her with his accusations. She'd been upset and angry that he could even think such things about her daughter.

'Devlin's moved to Wellington?' Shock filtered through the ether. 'I didn't think he'd ever leave his family.'

'You and me both. They're a unit that no one or anything breaches.' The calm disappeared as her stomach squeezed. 'But, Mum, did you hear me? He's joined the ED so we're now working together.' She stared up and down the beach, glaring at every male figure within sight. The way her day had unfolded, there was every possibility that at any moment Devlin would come sauntering along to relax after work, rubbing in how much her life had suddenly changed from the easy, comfortable way she'd made it since moving to Wellington. Where was he living?

Had he bought a house here? An apartment? It would be in one of the expensive suburbs. That was what he was used to and could afford without a blink. Since she was walking on the beach at Oriental Bay there was every likelihood he wasn't far away, this being one of the most prized areas to live in.

'This should prove interesting.' Laughter was not meant to be part of her mother's reply.

'Mum! You're supposed to be on my side. You know how much he hurt me.' Though today he'd been a gentleman most of the time.

'A lot can change in seven years, Chloe.' Her mother had become serious. Warning bells were sounding. 'Don't get too tied up in what went down back then. You've matured and found your own strengths. Be friends at least.'

'What? After what he accused me of? I don't think so.' She shouldn't have told her mum Devlin was in town. Wasn't she supposed to support her daughter no matter what? Except she had an odd feeling she couldn't explain that it was going to be too easy to get along with Devlin, like it or not.

'I know where you're coming from, sweetheart. I still want to tear strips off him for what he did, but it's a long time ago and dragging up those feelings again will only undermine and hurt you.'

'True.' Damn it.

'What was it like working with him?'

'Fine. Just like any other emergency doctor, he was on the ball and knew how to prioritise patients. He didn't waste time when it came to getting the help they needed.' Which showed she could at least do her job without the past causing friction. He was the type of doctor she liked working alongside. It was the first time they'd been together in an ED and he was as good as his reputation in Auckland suggested. If today was anything to go by she couldn't fault him as a doctor. An image of that tall, lean body as he bent down to lift Wendy Wright's plinth filled her head. Hard to find any fault there either.

Genie dropped a stick at her feet and sat back on her haunches, staring up at her with a pleading look in her eyes.

Bending down, Chloe rubbed Genie's head and picked up the stick. As she hurled it out over the water she pulled a face. Such a normal winter's early evening, she and Genie getting their exercise and fresh air, and yet her head and heart weren't quite so relaxed as usual. 'I can't help the memories he's stirred up, Mum.'

Not only the love she'd had for him, but of their baby. Had he received her message about her miscarriage? Or had he tossed the note she'd left in his letterbox in the bin without even reading it? By that point she hadn't bothered texting him as he'd already blocked her number. She'd been about seven weeks, unaware of the pregnancy, probably because of the trauma of breaking up with Devlin, and being horrendously busy at work. She'd been nursing on a children's ward where they'd been dealing with an outbreak of influenza. Plus she'd still not given up her other job at the supermarket as she'd wanted to pay off as fast as possible the loan she'd taken out to go to nursing school. Initially Devlin had tried to insist on paying it off for her, but she'd refused. It would've taken something away from her when she'd been so proud of her accomplishments.

'Naturally the memories are still there, but, as you've never seen or heard from Devlin since that night, this could bring about final closure for you.'

Closure. She hated that word. Whenever people said it she could hear a door slamming shut. It was as though a whole part of her life would be neatly excised and she wouldn't be able to recall the twenty months she'd known Devlin, which included love and fun and excitement, and the complete certainty he believed in her, saw her strengths and weaknesses and didn't care. That had been so important after the way men had treated her all her life, as if she were an appendage to her mother, or there to fetch and carry, as Stephen had made her feel. Also, her finals and the excitement of becoming a registered nurse, the most amazing thing she'd ever accomplished, were a part of that time with Devlin. Nor did she want to forget the embryo that had once been growing inside her, that had slipped away one cold, lonely night with a rush of pain and despair that had woken her in the middle of many nights since. 'Mum, I'll be all right. We got through today, so it's only going to get easier.' *I hope.* 'I'd better go. Genie is on a scent trail.'

Nose down, tail up, Genie was heading further along the beach towards the Italian restaurant where people were already sitting at tables in the window. Not a good sign. Genie always expected treats there, and often got them. But the big problem was the busy road between the beach and the restaurant. At least she was still well down the beach.

'Genie, stop, sit.'

Genie continued as if she hadn't heard.

Chloe jogged towards her dog, the lead swinging from her hand. 'Genie, stop, girl.'

With a flick of her tail, Genie finally obeyed.

'Good girl.' Clicking the lead onto Genie's collar, Chloe straightened up, and her breath

stuck in her throat as she came face to face
with Devlin.

'Hello, Chloe. Your dog's cute. What breed
is she?' Devlin stood a couple of metres away,
dressed in jeans with a white tee shirt and navy
wind jacket.

I just knew he'd be around here somewhere.

She coughed out the stalled air in her lungs.
'Genie's a mongrel.' Not a pure breed of any
kind.

A bit like me.

She didn't know who her father was, and,
since he'd walked away before she was even
born, she didn't have any longing to know him
either. If she hadn't been good enough for him
to hang around to meet her, then to hell with
him. Not that she'd reached that decision early
or easily, but these days she didn't waste energy
or emotion on people who didn't care about her.
'I got her from the rescue centre.'

'Looks like she's got some lab in her.' He
crouched down to hold out his hand for Genie
to sniff. 'Hey, girl.'

Genie obliged with her nose, then sat back to
allow Devlin to rub her between the shoulders.

Fickle girl.

Don't trust him. He'll hurt you.

'Most likely poodle and lab. She bounces
around like one and loves to eat like the other.'

And was the most affectionate creature in her life, Chloe admitted to herself. 'I got her a couple of years ago. She's the first pet I've ever had.' Why she'd waited so long to get a dog was beyond her. One of those things on her going-to-do list, along with a hundred other things she'd been slowly ticking off since she'd made it to Italy and found an inner strength she hadn't known she possessed.

Devlin stood up, watching her closely. 'I meant to get your phone number before we knocked off, but I got caught up and you were gone. Someone mentioned you usually walked your dog here and, since I live close by, I figured I'd try and catch up with you.'

That someone Jaz by any chance? 'I thought we dealt with the problem between us already.' Not that they'd actually aired their grievances.

He shrugged. 'I wasn't sure about how you felt, that's all.'

'Annoyed, if I'm honest. But there's no point raking over the past. It happened, and can't be undone. You're here, and we'll get along well enough for work.' Disappointment dragged at her. She wanted more? She flinched internally. Get out of here. Not likely. Why couldn't he have grown a pot belly and lost some of that thick dark hair?

'You seem settled. Happy.'

Where did that come from? Happy was not on her radar at this moment. She'd have to lie a little. 'I am both. It took a while but here I am, doing great.'

'Do you live around here?'

'Close. I bought a tiny two-bedroom cottage behind the theatre in Te Aro, which needs lots of maintenance I'm slowly making my way through.' Not far from here. It'd cost an arm and a leg, and she'd be paying off the mortgage till she was old and doddery, but it was hers, thanks to her stepdad backing her loan application. 'A couple of minutes' walk to Cuba Street and ten to the CBD. I mostly walk to work, too. Perfect really.'

His laugh was short and sharp. 'I'm in an apartment over the road. Near enough to Cuba Street, the CBD and the hospital, too.'

So she'd got the location right.

Their eyes met, locked. Who'd have thought it? It was funny that they'd both ended up in the same city, *and* the same hospital. Funny? Try again. More like strange. Though maybe not. New Zealand wasn't huge, and there weren't many big cities, which were the only places either of them would choose to live and work.

She looked away. Devlin's eyes were too intense to be dealing with. Once she'd loved that he could look at her like that. Not any more. He brought back memories of great times. He also made her shiver with something like longing, or was it regret? Of course, she regretted their break up, but that was long over, and there was nothing to rue now. Not even the fact that she couldn't get back with Devlin? Definitely not. If he'd been able to so easily believe she'd gone behind his back for sex then, no; she would never be ready to try again with him. 'Dev—' Damn it. 'Devlin, I'd better get going. I need to stop at the supermarket to get Genie something for dinner.'

Understanding filled his eyes. 'It isn't easy, is it?'

'You're right, it's not. But I'm not going over old territory. You wouldn't listen to me before. Why would you now?' Her pulse was deafening.

Devlin nodded. 'I don't want a rerun on the old argument, but we need to bury the hatchet so the past doesn't interfere in our daily lives. I don't think we quite got that far earlier.'

She stared at him for a long moment, and felt some of the tension back off. 'You're right on all counts. Today's brought everything back but I can deal with it. We'll get along just fine.' Because they had to. And because, 'It might be good for us.' Not sure how though.

'I'll walk to the end of the beach with you.'

Not quite what she wanted, but it was only a short distance, and maybe a step in the right direction as far as their new relationship went. 'All right. Come on, Genie.' She strode away, aware with each step she took that Devlin was right beside her. Her head spun. They might have to work together, but out here, away from their professional environment, she expected him to be heading in the opposite direction. Seemed Devlin was more comfortable around her than she was with him. Or more determined to knock out the elephant between them.

Minutes later they reached the roadside, and Chloe held her breath, waiting for Devlin's next move.

'See you tomorrow,' he said.

She nodded. 'Let's hope nothing too drastic occurs first thing. If at all.'

When she reached the other side of the busy road, she couldn't help glancing over her shoulder, and breathed deep.

Devlin stood with his hands on his hips, watching her. Devlin Walsh was back in her life. Not in the same way, but still a bubble burst inside her and tears welled up to spill down her cheeks.

I loved you so much, Devlin, how could you believe I'd hurt you like that?

Unbelievable. She was over him, yet still hurt

by the fact he'd never accepted her truth over what he'd thought had happened. Flicking her head forward, she strode out in the direction of the supermarket, her hand gripping Genie's lead like a lifeline. Genie was her reliable pal, happy as long as there was food in the bowl and a warm, dry bed to sprawl out on. How easy was that? Too easy?

Chloe owned a two-bed cottage a kilometre or two from his apartment. Did that mean she was single? Hadn't settled down with another man? Or she had and the relationship had gone belly up? She'd said she'd bought a house, not 'they' had. Devlin watched those long legs eating up the distance to the corner and remembered how she used to wind them around his waist when they made love. But it hadn't been love, had it? It had been sex, plain and simple, for Chloe. Love for him though.

Strange how today he'd had the strangest feeling something didn't ring true about their break up. By all appearances, she'd had another man on the side, just as his previous partner had. They'd both denied it, even when he'd caught them out. But there was a difference. Chloe hadn't been naked, nor in bed with the guy. She'd been quick to deny his allegations but he'd been so shocked, so hurt, that he hadn't wanted to fall for those lies again. He hadn't been able to put his finger on what, only that despite everything that had happened he was still attracted to her, could feel those too-familiar sparks of desire whenever he'd glanced at her today.

It wasn't as though there hadn't been other women since Chloe. He was a man with a healthy sexual appetite. But there hadn't been another woman he'd given his heart to. Not only because he didn't trust so readily any more—two women cheating on him was more than enough—but also because Chloe had touched him in a way he'd never entirely forgotten. She'd come into his life when they were both busy studying, and didn't have lots of free time to spend together, and they'd made the most of every opportunity to be together, and then made some more because they couldn't stay away from each other. Then he'd proposed. Chloe had burst into tears of happiness and cried yes so loud he'd have been surprised if half of Auckland hadn't heard. Her reaction had filled him with more love than he'd believed possible. It was for ever; he'd found his other half. He'd been hurt once before but with Chloe it had been like coming home, having found that special place where he'd always be safe. It just showed how badly he read women. Cath had hurt him. Chloe had sliced him in half.

Devlin took one last look at her, swallowing the longing that rose in his throat before turning around to walk the other way. How could he possibly want Chloe? Why? What was there about her that possessed him so wholly that his body ached for her, his head grew light when watching her work with a patient, his heart squeezed when she rubbed her dog's head? One day working with her, and he was in an unbelievable mess. He, who could handle death before his eyes at work without losing his sanity, could not catch up with his ex-fiancée without feeling as though the floor had disappeared beneath his feet. So much for thinking moving to Wellington would be straightforward. If only he'd known she lived here. Then what? He would still have moved here because he'd believed he was over her.

But was he? Or was his love buried so deep he couldn't feel or taste it? Had she, by repeating what Cath had done, made him feel worthless when it came to giving his heart away? Did women really only want him for his status and wealth? It had seemed as though that had been the last thing Chloe had her eye on when they got together. She'd appeared genuinely uninterested in his family's position in society, only in him. Though not enough if she could play around behind his back. If? Of course she had. He still saw that man strutting around her flat semi-naked, a smirk on his face that had Dev wanting to punch him. What if he'd been wrong though? Chloe had been quick to say he was. So had Cath in his previous relationship and she'd only proven he should accept the truth when it was right before his eyes. She'd lied. Likewise Chloe. Hadn't she? Of course she had.

Hadn't she?

His strides lengthened as frustration welled up. He'd have to take things one day at a time. Tomorrow he'd work alongside Chloe again and it would get easier. By the end of the week he'd probably be wondering what the hiccup had been about.

Except the moment Devlin walked into the ED at six-fifty the next morning his heart did a dance. Chloe was already reading patient notes on the computer while sipping tea, a furrow between her eyes, an intense expression tightening her face.

'What's up?' he asked, pulling out a seat beside her.

'Morning, Dev. I mean, Devlin,' she added hurriedly, a pretty shade of pink colouring her cheeks.

He leaned back on the chair. 'What've we

got?' He'd thought he'd been early but Chloe had beaten him here.

'Forty-three-year-old man, broken ribs and punctured lung, waiting for surgery. They've got him on a regime of morphine and tramadol.' She flicked the screen, moved down through the files. 'Twenty-five-year-old woman, thirty-one weeks pregnant, eclampsia. She's going to the neonatal unit shortly.'

As Chloe continued to outline their cases, Devlin absorbed her calm attitude. She was good; no doubt about it. She talked about the patients clearly and with an understanding of the data. She didn't get wound up about the severity of the cases they saw in zone three, just told him like it was. But if he still knew anything about Chloe, she'd be hurting for her patients behind that steady face. It was in her DNA. There'd been times when he'd held her while she'd downloaded her sorrow for someone she'd been nursing. He couldn't see why that would've changed. Chloe had known hardship growing up and with that came an empathy for others not doing so well. Yet she'd hurt him.

But had she? What if he'd reacted too quickly? Hadn't listened to her pleas all because of what Cath had done? Not once did he stop and think he might be wrong. Instead he'd turned his back—and his heart—on her. Now he realised there'd never been a glimmer of guilt in her eyes any time she'd looked at him back then, or yesterday.

The pen he'd been holding dropped to the floor.

What? Of course she'd betrayed him. He'd been told she was having a fling with another trainee nurse on the ward where she was working. A guy with a reputation of enjoying all the fresh-faced nurses. His mother had been adamant Chloe had been seen with him, and she'd been backed up by one of Dev's female colleagues.

One who his mother had later tried to get him to date.

He hadn't thought of that before, had he? But he had also seen Chloe and the man together having coffee at a café along the road from the hospital. Chloe had been laughing and talking as though she didn't have a care in the world. It had been so obvious what had happened when he'd found the guy in her flat, strutting around in nothing but a towel after a shower.

What if he'd been wrong jumping to that conclusion? Maybe Chloe hadn't done anything wrong. It might've been true the man's hot water system had failed.

But his mother wouldn't lie to him. She might

not have thought Chloe would be the ideal daughter-in-law, but she'd never deliberately set out to hurt him by lying about something so important, not when she knew he'd already been cheated on with the first love of his life.

'Devlin, the ambulance is here,' Chloe called out.

How the hell was he supposed to focus on a patient with these crazy thoughts tripping around his head? Suck it up and get on with what was important right now. That was how. 'Coming.'

The paramedics were rolling the bed into Resus where Chloe waited, ready to help shift their patient across to the hospital bed before replacing the ambulance monitor with the department's one.

Devlin strode up, his professional face firmly in place, and one of the paramedics handed him the notes he'd made of readings and the description of the woman's pain, which suggested heart problems. Must be something in Wellington's water bringing on heart attacks first thing in the morning. He gave a tight smile. 'Tell me what's going on.'

'Pain in the chest woke me up.' The woman, Iris, by the notes, answered tearfully. 'Like really bad pain in my left side and arm. I thought I was going to die.'

Nurse Chloe touched the back of Iris's hand. 'You're here now, and we've got everything covered. That's what matters at this point.' Nurse and caring woman all in one, he thought with a wince.

Devlin focused on the monitor, noting the arrhythmia that suggested ventricular fibrillation. Iris could've had a heart attack this morning, one that hadn't been strong enough to stop her heart but could still do a lot of damage all the same.

Jaz stepped into Resus, said quietly, 'Devlin, got a minute? We've got a patient bleeding heavily via the throat.'

'I'll be right there.' He scanned the monitors, read the notes, knew there was nothing he could actively do for the woman as long as nothing changed in her readouts. She needed a cardiologist to pay her a visit. 'Iris, I'm calling the cardiology department to get a specialist to see you. In the meantime, just do as Chloe tells you and you'll be fine.' Following Jaz, he asked, 'Is the patient coughing?'

'Some deep bellied air gasps rather than coughing.' Jaz slipped around a curtain at cubicle three. 'Judy, Hugo, this is Devlin, one of our doctors.'

Devlin acknowledged the man, presumably the husband, then dipped his head to Judy, the woman clinging to Hugo's hand. 'When did the bleeding start, Judy?'

The woman croaked, 'About three hours ago.'

Jaz wiped her mouth and chin.

Devlin continued. 'To save you talking and causing more bleeding I'll ask Hugo the details. Is that all right?'

'Yes,' Judy whispered.

At least that was what he thought she said, as she'd barely opened her mouth. 'Is Judy suffering any pain?'

'Yes, she told the paramedic it was six out of ten, but knowing Judy it's probably more than that. She's a tough old girl.'

Judy blinked rapidly.

Hugo smiled endearingly. 'Okay, not old.' He tapped his chest on the right side. 'She indicated it hurt most here. Her throat was sore last night, and still is, I think.'

Judy nodded.

'Has she suffered sore throats a lot recently? Had the flu or a cold in the last month?'

'No.'

Jaz looked at Devlin, and inclined her head towards the monitor, which just then beeped at a level that was a warning. The blood pressure was thirty-five, too low. 'Any history of low blood pressure?'

'No, the opposite. She's on tablets to lower it. I don't know what it used to be.'

'Fair enough.' A lot of people didn't really understand BP readings clearly. 'I'll look up her medical history online. I can access her medical-centre data.' Thank goodness for easy access these days. It saved lots of time on phones waiting for people to verify who he was and then going into details. 'Judy, I'm going to look at your chest and tap the area where Hugo said the pain was.'

Jaz helped lift the woman's shirt and covered her abdomen with a cotton blanket for decency.

She was good, as good as Chloe. But she *wasn't* Chloe. Already he preferred working with Chloe, even when only minutes ago he'd been in a hurry to put space between them. As it had been years ago, when he'd enjoyed being with her all the time. A tingling warmth and a lightness in his heart had always been present. Weird how it had returned now whenever they were in the same room.

No, he was over her.

Judy gasped when he pressed below her rib-cage on the right. And again when he pressed further towards her abdomen. There was no re-action when he did the same on the left. 'Judy, I'd like you to roll onto your left side.'

Jaz helped the woman. 'That's it. Lie still.'

More pain was apparent when Devlin tested her back. 'Right, you can lie on your back again.' Popping the stethoscope buds into his ears, he said, 'Breathe deep, hold it. Let it out slowly.' He repeated the move three times over different regions of Judy's lungs, before tossing his gloves into the bin. 'I'm going to arrange an X-ray of your chest, specifically your lungs. I think there's fluid on your lungs.'

'That's where the blood's coming from?' Judy asked with dread in her eyes.

'Possibly, or your throat is raw and bleeding. But more likely it's the lungs. I'll also arrange some blood tests. I want to see if you've got an infection going on in there.'

Hugo reached for his wife's hand and held tight. 'We'll be all right, Jude.'

Heading to the hub, Devlin glanced over to Iris's cubicle, saw Chloe giving her a dose of medication, no doubt the painkiller he'd ordered. Calm, steady Chloe.

Hell, I've missed her.

Shock rippled through him. That was nonsense. He hadn't even thought about her very often, deliberately burying her for ever. That had created a void within himself he hadn't understood, had put down to losing two women to other men, and feeling he wasn't quite good enough to keep a woman at his side for ever. He hadn't believed that void was about not having Chloe sharing his life, laughing, crying, loving with him. Now she was nearby, within sight and touching distance, he was remembering a lot of things about her he'd always loved. Her soft smile that unravelled the knots forming in his belly after a particularly difficult day at work. The way her right eyebrow rose slightly higher than the left when she was puzzled by something. The irritation that darkened the caramel shade of her eyes to mahogany whenever she felt she'd inadvertently let him or his family down. The soft shade of pink polish she wore on her nails—except now she wore bright orange. But there was a strong tilt to her chin, a straightness of her spine that hadn't been there before. The void was filling in a little.

'Have you phoned upstairs?' she was asking now, reminding him what he was supposed to be doing, which didn't include daydreaming about something that had run its course.

'About to. Any changes I need to know about?'

'Everything's steady.' Her focus was firmly on their patient.

Devlin felt as though he was being given the cold shoulder, but knew he was imagining it. There was no reason for her to act that way. Anyway, she wouldn't do that around here when there were colleagues and patients in all directions. She had no reason apart from their break up and him accusing her of cheating on him. Even frost dissipated after a time. Now he was being sarcastic, not his usual stance. Anyway, it was himself he was uncomfortable with today, not Chloe. That new niggling question about whether he'd been right to believe what he'd heard and supposedly thought he'd seen. 'I'll be back shortly.' He refrained from saying she was doing a good job. It would sound condescending when really he was looking for something to say that was genuine and friendly.

The tension tightened more and more over the day so that Devlin started clock-watching for the end of his shift to come round so he could get away from the stifling air that went wherever Chloe went. Air he had to share and breathe every minute.

'Chloe, you're needed in Reception.' Kirsty, the receptionist, rushed into the centre of the department. 'There's an elderly man and his wife and they can't speak English well enough to get the info we need. They're Italian.'

Was Chloe fluent enough to interpret for the couple? Wow.

'Coming. Jaz, can you keep an eye on our patients for a mo?' Chloe was heading away without waiting for an answer, obviously used to this.

'Need me out there?' Devlin followed the women.

'You speak Italian, too?' Kirsty asked.

'Not a word.'

'Then no, we've got it.'

'Fine.' He stopped outside the last cubicle before Reception. Obviously he hadn't put two and two together. Naturally Chloe would have learned at least enough Italian to get through the day-to-day tasks with the family she'd lived with.

He heard Chloe say, *'Quando e iniziato il dolore?'* then pause and say, 'Two hours.' Then, *'Su una scalada uno a due, dieci al massimo, quanto e forte il dolore?'* She listened, then, 'Eight.'

He was gobsmacked. Chloe wasn't hesitant over her choice of words, talking and pausing to listen to replies, giving Kirsty the answers without breaking for air. Just like an Italian. Okay, maybe not quite as rapidly, but pretty darned close. Who was this Chloe? Certainly not one he'd known, or loved, or been going to marry. The surprises just kept on coming. Impressive.

'Grazie.' Chloe was heading his way, a cheeky

smile lightening her face. 'Surprised you, huh?' Her shoulder bumped his upper arm.

'You certainly have.' He nudged back. 'Go, you.'

She sucked a quick breath, muttered, 'Right. Where was I?' and disappeared around a cubicle curtain.

He headed back into the hub, shaking his head and grinning to himself. This woman was interesting. No wonder he couldn't put her aside. She was becoming a challenge. *A what?* He didn't need any challenges, and certainly not from Chloe. She was already pushing his buttons in far too many ways, and yes, he had to admit he was intrigued. He could remember how it felt being in love with her, to spend time with her in mutually enjoyable activities. He'd given her his heart within a matter of days, and she'd reciprocated. As if they were meant to be together for ever. It had felt wonderful being loved beyond anything he'd known before, to feel wanted for himself. They'd become inseparable very quickly, yet it had all turned to dust even faster.

Now he wondered who she really was, and he felt those old, familiar pricks of desire and longing all over again. With so many questions turning over in his mind, he had to find time to spend with her to ask them, to discover if he'd been wrong seven years ago. Looking around, he realised how quiet the department had become. Nothing urgent required his attention in zone three. 'Up for a coffee?' he asked Chloe. Seemed they were forever meeting over patients or going for coffee. 'I know it's not long till knock-off but we deserve one.'

Her eyebrows rose as she looked around. 'Might as well while we can. Who knows what's about to arrive?'

The speed at which they left the hub made Devlin feel like a naughty boy playing hooky, half expecting to be called back for a patient. It was fun.

With steaming mugs in hand, they sat at a table in the corner of the cafeteria and sighed simultaneously.

'What a morning,' Chloe groaned. 'Non-stop patients.'

'Then you were prattling away in another language. How cool is that? How would those people have coped without you there?'

She stared at him for a moment, then all of a sudden she beamed. 'I'm not the only person working in the hospital who speaks Italian. There's a strong Italian community in the region. But I do get a buzz whenever I get to help out.'

'I bet you do.' She looked pleased with herself. 'Guess that trip to Europe has a lot to answer for. You're more confident now, too.'

'When you're in the middle of Rome and no one understands you, and you need to find a loo in a hurry, then you learn fast.' She laughed.

Dev sipped his coffee and relaxed in the chair. What more could he want?

CHAPTER FOUR

'Do WE REALLY have to go for a walk?' Chloe stared down at Genie, sitting expectantly in front of her, the lead hanging from her teeth. There were days Chloe was so exhausted after work that the last thing she wanted was to go for a walk, but it usually turned out for the best. If Genie didn't bring the lead to her on those days and get her outside into the fresh air, then she'd mooch around getting bored and fed up with herself. Patting Genie's head, she laughed. 'Okay, you win. Again.'

Genie did a circle on the spot, understanding full well she'd won, as she always did.

'You're good for me, aren't you?' Another pat.

Another circle, Genie's tail waving all over the place.

'Watch out.' Chloe caught the water bottle that had been on the coffee table before it landed on the carpet. 'We'll go up the hill today.' If Devlin decided to go to the beach, she didn't want to bump into him.

She needed a break from those intense blue eyes that seemed to watch her every move. She wasn't sure if he was sizing her up as a nurse or his ex, or as someone he wanted to work side by side with and not worry about the past coming back to bite him on the backside. Much how she felt. Time to drop the past and move on? Again? This time jointly, without the hurt tainting everything? Why not? Nothing to be gained holding onto the pain.

After changing into black jeans and a warm top, she let her hair down from the messy bun she wore for work and brushed out the knots, trying to shove away the unusual tiredness that sat over her. It had been a busy, but normal day in the department, if she could call working alongside the man she'd once given her heart to normal. Well, it was becoming her new normal. Of course, she wouldn't always be rostered on the same shift as him, but the doctors tended to stay on after theirs was finished, not rushing to leave particularly ill patients until the next doctors on duty were ready to take over. Spending eight hours in the same department, with the same medical staff and patients, meant they were part of a team. Something she'd once had with Devlin in her private life.

Three days together, and already she wanted to get beyond the past so they were connected, if only as medical colleagues and in their thinking and approach to patients. Something they already seemed to be doing.

They'd once matched perfectly in a lot of other ways. Relaxing on the deck with a glass of wine at the end of a hard day at their respective jobs, unwinding by talking over the things that had distressed them. Similar quirky things that made them laugh until their sides ached. Sleeping in late when they had a day off, waking with their legs entwined and Dev's hand splayed across her stomach. Knowing how to touch each other while making love, bringing each other to a climax and kissing until the world spun.

But he hadn't truly understood her, hadn't been on the same page as her when she'd denied having sex with another man. It was still hard to forgive as it said he hadn't known her as well as she'd believed. To be so ready to believe the worst, not wanting to stop and listen to her, not once, suggested she'd never had a chance to prove that it was beyond her to do what Cath had inflicted on him. Almost as if he'd wanted to believe the worst. From that moment on they'd had nothing in common. Except broken hearts. They'd been deeply hurt. *Both* of them. And still, despite that, she liked what she'd seen of Devlin so far this week. Her heart did anyway, getting in a pickle at times, totally out of sync with her head, which kept reminding her she hadn't done anything wrong and, therefore, he didn't deserve her as any more than a professional colleague. But, said her heart way too often, he was still incredibly gorgeous and kind and sexy. Down, heart, down.

Genie gave her a not too gentle head-butt on her knee. *Come on, Mum.*

'Sorry, girl. Got a lot on my mind.' Shoving her wallet, keys and phone in her bum bag, she closed the door behind them and headed down the path, sunglasses and cap in place. The sun was heading towards the horizon but she never went without her glasses. 'We'll have early dinner with the boys after this.'

Wednesday nights she went to the Italian restaurant across from the beach for a meal and a catch up with brothers, Giuseppe and Lorenzo. They'd treated her like a sister ever since the day she'd been passing the restaurant and heard a man yelling for help. Inside Lorenzo had been holding a severely burned arm under the cold tap and Giuseppe had been running round in circles unsure what to do. Talking calmly in Italian, getting Giuseppe to close the restaurant and get his car ready, she'd examined the damage. Large blisters had formed over the back of Lorenzo's hand and up his arm, but it was the raw redness between his fingers that had given her concern, so she'd taken over and driven the men to the ED where Lorenzo had got the necessary care and hadn't lost too many days behind his ovens in the restaurant.

Out of the gate, Genie pulled in the direction of the beach.

'No, girl, we're going this way.' Chloe tugged gently and began striding out along the path towards the track that led to the hill, feeling a wee bit mean.

Going this way wasn't as much fun for Genie as she had to remain on the lead instead of being able to run around free on the beach, chasing gulls and leaping into the water. Instead they'd go further than planned, and get a little bit tired, before going to the waterfront for dinner. The guys always had a bowl of treats for Genie, which she lapped up with a wagging tail to show her appreciation.

'I wonder what tonight's special is on the menu.' Not that it mattered. She ate anything Lorenzo cooked.

A woman going in the opposite direction gave her a funny look, and shook her head.

Chloe didn't slow down. It didn't count as talking to herself if Genie was there, right?

All the way up the hill, and down another way through the large homes to reach Oriental Parade, Devlin was firmly on her mind. He just would not go away. Her hands tightened and loosened. How could he do this to her after so long? Hey, was she having the same effect on him? Now there was a thought. That'd make them two sad puppies, for certain. Very sad.

Her phone rang.

Devlin.

'Hi. What are you up to?' Did she sound too friendly?

'I'm heading to the beach to stretch my legs.'

Those long, muscular legs. Right. Her mouth dried.

'I was wondering if you were there already and if I could join you for a bit?'

Don't bring your legs. They'll distract me from any sane thought I might have.

'We've been up the hill, but Genie's not done yet so more exercise on the beach wouldn't go astray.'

'Great. See you in a bit.'

Great? Yes, it actually was. He was hanging out in her head all the time anyway, so why not spend time with the real deal, possibly iron out some of the kinks in their new relationship?

When she reached the water's edge, Chloe picked up a stick to hurl out over the water and promptly got soaked as Genie leapt after it. 'Thanks, my girl. Remind me not to do you any favours for a while.'

'Bet she does that to you all the time.' Devlin bloody Walsh. Why couldn't he have called out hello from further away instead of being so close?

She spun around so fast she lost her balance and would've landed on her butt if Devlin hadn't caught her arm.

'Steady. I didn't mean to scare you.'

'You didn't.' Much. More like morphed from an image in her head to a full-on, tall, sexy, *real* man still holding her arm. Pulling sharply, she freed her arm and took a step back. 'You couldn't.'

A small, lopsided smile appeared. 'I know. You never scared easily.'

She laughed, surprising herself. 'Unless there's lightning about.' Once, as a kid, she'd seen lightning strike a tree that sheep had been sheltering under. The ensuing mess had stayed with her ever since.

'I can see you've toughened up even more.' He wasn't smiling any more.

'I sure have.' This conversation was all too serious, too soon.

Genie dropped the stick on her foot.

Saved by her fur baby. Rubbing Genie's head,

she threw the stick again, and got splashed once more. 'I'm a slow learner.'

Dev laughed.

And her gut went all gooey. Over a laugh? A sexy, friendly, nothing-bad-meant laugh.

He said, 'That's not how I would've described you.'

She wasn't falling for that one. She did not need to know how he'd describe her. His last, loud, harsh opinion of her was all too easy to recall despite all the time in between.

Devlin reached for the stick hanging out of Genie's jaw. 'Give me that and let's see how far I can throw it.'

As they strolled along the beach, chatting about next to nothing, Chloe snuggled into herself, letting the warmth of her jersey and this easy camaraderie take over. Just how it used to be.

'What are you doing after your walk?' Devlin asked as they retraced their steps once Genie was worn out.

She turned to look at him. 'Why?'

His chest rose on an inhale as he looked at her. 'Want to have dinner with me at that Italian restaurant over the road?'

Devlin waited, a breath stalled in the back of his throat. Where had that come from? He'd only intended a bit of time together on the beach, working slowly at chiselling away the past, finding the good things that had been part of their relationship, and then only enough to put their history away where it belonged.

'I don't know, Dev.'

Dev. Did she realise that over the last three days she'd sometimes reverted to her pet name for him? A name he'd loved, because it made him feel special, hers, and no one else's. His mother had loathed it, saying they'd named him Devlin. 'Why?' Relief should be pouring through him at her hesitancy, not this disappointment. 'I thought it might be a good way to clear the air a bit more.' Did he? At the rate he was going, he should become a storyteller.

One well-shaped eyebrow rose slowly.

He'd forgotten that move, and how it made him laugh. Except he wasn't laughing now. He wanted to sit down over a meal with Chloe and talk to her about life in general, not only work. What she had been doing throughout the years since they'd split, other than going overseas. He wanted to know more about that, too. What had changed her mind about travelling to the other side of the world where everything would be new to her? For a year at that. So much to learn and he couldn't wait to start finding out. 'What do you say?'

A red hue touched her cheeks. 'I'm already eating there tonight.'

'Oh.' His chest tightened. There was someone else in her life. Should've known. Because she was gorgeous and wouldn't be without someone special at her side. 'Fair enough.'

She slipped her sunglasses off and glared. As if he was frustrating her. 'Oh, damn it, Devlin. Okay, we'll share a table.'

He was none the wiser. Did that mean she would be alone? Or that others would be there? One other? 'I don't want to intrude.' But he did want to spend time with Chloe, make it possible to work together without the tightening in his gut, his groin, and even his heart that occurred on and off throughout their shifts.

The dog had returned with the stick and was shaking saltwater everywhere.

'Stop that, Genie,' Chloe growled through a smile, before rubbing her pet's head. 'The brothers who own the restaurant are friends and I eat there regularly. So does Genie—though she gets to sit outside the back door on her own special mat.' She drew a breath and locked formidable eyes on him. 'Yes, let's have dinner together, and, as you said, continue clearing the air. Though I don't think we've done too badly so far.' That eyebrow lifted again, then fell back into place.

'I guess being on the job, and being professional, has its place.' He tried for a smile of his own and surprised himself at how easily it came. 'When were you going to the restaurant?'

Another blush coloured her tanned cheeks red. 'When we're done here. I took Genie up the hill so she's had her walk. I was just letting her have a bit more fun.'

He didn't quite believe her but couldn't work out what was missing in that explanation. Leaving it alone, Devlin held out his hand for the stick. 'I'll throw that for her.'

Watching Genie race into the water without a care brought back a longing for a dog of his own. It was something he'd put off because he was never home enough, and now he was living in an apartment it would be totally unfair. No back yard to run around in, having to be stuck inside all day except for walks, was not how a dog should live. Especially a large dog, which was what he'd like.

'She's so good for me,' Chloe said. 'On days like today when I'm exhausted and all I want to do is sit down with a coffee and unwind she makes me go for a walk, which is what I need all along.'

'Bet you talk to her, too.'

'All the time. We have the most interesting conversations and I'm never wrong.'

'You don't say?' Picking up the stick Genie had dropped in front of him, he hurled it along the beach. 'Let's get some of that water off you, Genie.'

Chloe shoved her hands in her pockets and watched Genie dash along the beach, sending sprays of sand left and right. 'What made you decide to move to Wellington?'

Crunch went his gut. 'It was time for a change.' There was no straightforward answer. Not when it was Chloe asking. She knew how his and Patrick's parents made so many demands on their time and life choices. He wasn't ready to bring up any of that yet. *But* he had instigated this. *And* there was the possibility talking about it, however briefly, might make him even happier he'd taken back control of his life.

Her head tilted to the side, and her lips twisted. 'Interesting.'

She knew his family and how everyone had their role, which included living in Auckland, especially in the correct suburb, being available for certain dinners or cocktail parties. 'Not as interesting as you might think. I was restless, and getting more so by the day. Moving overseas seemed the perfect solution but it didn't enthuse me. Not sure why, but when a mate from training days phoned to say there was a position down here I got quite excited, which told me I should look closer.' The truth, just not all of it.

'So here you are.'

'Yep.'

'Glad you moved?'

'So far.' Had she just let him get away with such a brief explanation? 'Yes.' Of all the hospitals in the country, or the world come to that, here he was, working in the same department as Chloe. Chloe, who'd agreed to join him for dinner. No denying the flicker of excitement in his gut. He felt something for Chloe, which might be wrong, but was true all the same. Was it wrong to feel like this after all this time? Did relationships get second chances? And the big question—were they worth the risk? But, hey, he'd had his heart broken twice and wasn't exactly on top of the world when it came to the love stakes so it might be an idea to have another crack at finding true love.

Looking at her, seeing that face that used to follow him into sleep every night with a twinkle in her eyes, knowing how she liked to walk for kilometres at a time and to hang her washing using matching-coloured pegs for each item, how too much coffee made her hyper and her shoes were always lined up perfectly in the wardrobe, was touching him in ways he'd never have thought possible. This woman had been his fiancée, the love of his life, and he'd not come close to a similar feeling with another woman since their horrible break up. He'd believed he'd got over her. Now it felt as if she'd been waiting deep within him, ready to leap out and take his hand to lead him somewhere he dared not even name.

'It's kind of different being in a far smaller city than Auckland. Everything seems to be central—everything I require or like anyway,' he said a little gruffly.

'Apart from getting away from people, that is, but even then it's not a long ride to find a less populated beach or hills to hike in. Even better, you can catch the ferry to go across to Picton and suss out the Marlborough Sounds or the vineyards. For me, Mum's close yet not so close.'

'She still likes to keep an eye on you?' Devlin laughed. Joy never hovered but she always had tabs on what Chloe was up to. When he commented one day, Chloe said her mum had been like that from the day she was born and she'd had to go it alone as a parent. If only his parents had been the same with him and his brother, and not quite so demanding of them to partake in lives neither of them wanted. Sure, he understood there were obligations to being wealthy, but to have his parents think they could decide on the right woman or career position for their sons made everything awkward and often downright exasperating. And the way his mother had treated Chloe back then had made his blood boil, but he'd been wasting his breath whenever he'd tried to talk to her about it.

'Not as much as she used to. Not that I'd change anything. She's always been a great mum, even if I used to fight with her a lot as a teen. Which was normal, I guess. Jack still supports me like I'm his daughter.' There was a lot of love in her voice, making his gut squeeze.

Chloe had always worn her heart on her sleeve. He'd forgotten that. Now a picture of the distress and pain in her face when he'd accused her of cheating on him appeared in his mind. She'd been devastated. He'd supposed that was because she'd been caught out. Not once did he consider she was hurting because *he'd* broken *her* heart. It had been all about the pain he'd been suffering. *Another* woman had done the dirty on him. He'd offered Chloe his heart and future, and she'd shown little respect or care for either. Or so he'd thought. Had he been wrong? Had he? No. Another picture of a muscular man wearing nothing but a towel wrapped around his waist and a knowing smirk on his mouth, standing in Chloe's lounge, came to mind.

Stop this. Or say sorry, you can't make dinner after all.

Because if these thoughts and images continued popping up then they were going to have an awful time at the restaurant.

He couldn't do it. He wanted to spend time with her.

Devlin looked along the beach, searching for Genie. Anything to distract him, help him get back on track. The dog was sitting quietly, letting a small girl pat her. 'Genie's quite placid, isn't she?'

'Unless there's a bone, or ball, or a warm bed on a cold day involved, then yes, mostly.'

They walked along in a companionable silence, Devlin keeping his mind under control. And his hormones. Sort of, anyway. They seemed to react around Chloe all too often. More memories? No. He wasn't going there. 'Why did you choose Italy instead of France or Britain or Spain?'

A soft smile lit up her face. 'Jack convinced me to get away for a while, and when I remained hesitant he bulldozed me by setting it all up with a family he'd met when he did his OE as a twenty-year-old. I'm so glad. It was truly the best experience I've had.'

'As you know, like others I trained with, I considered going overseas for my junior doctor years, but it didn't happen. Too many other things going on, I guess. Or I wasn't as keen as I'd thought.'

Chloe glanced at him from under her fringe. 'We were together then and planning a wedding.' There was no apology or sorrow in her voice.

Nor did he feel any. He'd finally come to accept it was what it was. These days it was the future that was disconcerting. 'It's not as if I didn't travel enough growing up.' He gave a bitter laugh. 'Mostly to resorts and cities with stunning sights to see that were on every traveller's to-visit list. Not quite the same as hunkering down in a hospital working all hours. Or doing what you did. That's truly amazing.'

'It was. You did what was right for you. That's what counts.' She stopped and called out. 'Genie, come.'

Genie trotted towards them, sniffing the air and wagging her tail.

'She's had enough.' Chloe clipped the lead onto her collar. 'Time for dinner, eh, girl?'

Genie nudged Chloe's thigh.

I did what was right for me.

Yes, Chloe was right, he had. Though now he was starting to think he might've been a bit short-sighted about missing the opportunity. At the time, because he was hurting so badly, he hadn't wanted to go to another country. To him, that would have felt like running away, and that was the last thing he'd ever do. 'A lot of junior doctors head offshore for extra experiences and they say it looks good on their CVs, but I can't say I've been held back for not going away.'

'Surely it comes down to how well you do your work? What you're like as a doctor.'

'I guess.' Not once had he missed out on a position he'd applied for, so he must've got something right, and presumably that was because he did know what he was doing and hopefully was better than good. 'I'm still as passionate about what I do as I was the day I qualified.' Talk about spilling his guts, but then this was Chloe, who he'd always told his true feelings to about anything from work to what he'd had for dinner. She'd listened to him, never brushed him aside. Unlike his parents. Stepping up as the next Walsh generation representative in the family business, and every other organisation they had anything to do with, was their choice, not his or Patrick's. They'd both been happy to contribute but wanted to get on with their careers and other things. Their lives, basically. 'You're much the same. You were going to become a top-notch nurse no matter what hurdles came your way, and you did it.'

Beginning to walk back the way they'd come, she peered up at him with a wonky smile lighting up her face. 'Even when bed pans made me nauseous and sticking needles into someone had my stomach in a knot.'

Laughter bubbled up through him. 'Find me a medical person who hasn't had their gremlins to deal with along the way. At least mine wasn't the sight of blood.'

'That only happens in the movies.' She laughed. 'But you didn't like straightening broken bones.'

He shuddered. 'Still don't, if I'm being honest, but I've learnt to deal with it while not doing any further damage or adding to the pain of my patient.'

'What's Patrick up to?'

'Living in Melbourne, married with a child on the way, and happier than he's been in a long time.' And not likely to ever return to Auckland and the family fold. Too much to lose, he reckoned. Already there was a lightness in his own step from being in a different city, different space. Yet the phone rang constantly with his mother demanding his presence for a charity function in Auckland. Like tonight. She'd expected him to fly back for a mayoral dinner. He'd turned her down, which hadn't made him popular. Tough. He wouldn't risk flying back in the morning and being late for his real job.

'Patrick's going to be a dad? Wow, that's great.' Chloe looked a little startled. 'Who'd have believed it?'

Of course, she'd remember his brother. They'd got along well, though she'd never agreed with all the gambling and drinking Patrick had done. 'He's calmed down a lot over the last few years.' Tell her? Why not? She shouldn't be too surprised. 'Patrick became addicted to his gambling. Dad put a hold on all his finances, told him to go away and sort himself out or he'd never get another cent.'

Chloe winced, her eyes widening. 'No support, then?'

She'd know the answer to that. Their parents believed in tough love, no holds barred. Which included not showing their feelings, though sometimes he got a sense there was a lot of love being held back. 'Mum and Dad don't like showing any softness towards us in case it makes us weak.'

'Don't I know it?'

Here they were, back to the past and their broken feelings. 'Chloe—'

'Dev, stop.' Her hand wrapped around his wrist. 'That was rude, I'm sorry. But I never believed your parents were affectionate towards you or Patrick, so if Patrick was crying out for help he was in big trouble.'

The problem with having started this conversation was Chloe did know his family better than most. She'd had to put up with criticism and expectations she had no idea how to handle. 'The good side to this is Patrick's found his feet and is making a solid career in finance, and he's happy with everything in his life. He left the country determined never to gamble again, and to stop drinking. He's done both, with a lot of support from Rachel, his wife.'

'I'm glad.'

Did she just mutter, 'One down, one to go'? He wasn't asking. He didn't need saving from anything. He was in charge of his own life and getting on with it very well, thank you very much. 'So am I. Now what are we likely to find on the menu at this restaurant?' Time to go with ordinary and easy.

'It's a small selection, only ten dishes, but each one is superb. Lorenzo keeps the prices down as his aim is to entice anyone and everyone to the restaurant to show them what Italian food is all about. He isn't interested in being a top restaurant that everyone must go to. He says it's about replicating his mother's kitchen back in Milan where all the relatives got together for a meal at least once a week.'

'I've not eaten Italian often.'

'You're not one of the it's-only-flour-and-water brigade, referring to pasta, are you?' There was that laughter again. She used to laugh a lot, but it had often been tight and full of concern that she'd got something wrong. Now it came easily and lightly, a happy sound.

'Guilty as charged.'

'So why choose there?'

'Because I saw the restaurant when I came along to the beach and when I suggested we have a meal together it seemed ideal. I also remembered how much you enjoyed pasta,' he admitted.

She blinked, glanced quickly at him and then away. 'I'd eat it all the time if only I could get off my backside and make some. The packet variety doesn't come up to scratch.'

'You still haven't taken up cooking in a big way?'

'Moved beyond the tinned soups and baked beans on toast? Not much. Though occasionally I try to put something together to share with friends. They usually suggest phoning out for something more edible.'

Friends. Not someone special, then. His step lightened. 'Cooking was never your forte. I still like to play around with flavours and proteins.

Gives me a sense of accomplishment when I create a tasty morsel.'

'I prefer eating to cooking.' She laughed. 'Let's cross the road while there's a gap in traffic.' She stopped on the footpath, and Genie sat. 'Good girl.' A flick of the lead and they were off.

Dev followed, watching those firm legs striding ahead with the dog beside her. He *had* missed Chloe. There'd been a big hole in his life that he hadn't been able to fill, and now he knew what had caused it. Despite what had happened, all along he'd been lonely without Chloe at his side.

This working-together business was causing all sorts of memories and longings that he'd never believed possible to resurface. Like right now he'd love a hug. Glancing at Chloe, his arms ready to wrap around her, he hesitated. Too soon. If ever appropriate. They were barely on the same page. *Yet.* They used to get along so well he could always grab a hug, give her a kiss, without hesitation. Yes, Devlin. A hug maybe. Kisses? Never. They belonged in the past.

Chloe headed up the side of the restaurant building, Genie's tail wagging faster than ever. 'We go through the back door,' she said over her shoulder. 'At least I do. Genie has her own spot on the back veranda.'

Dev followed. 'Their most regular customers, then?'

'Possibly.' Lorenzo and Giuseppe were going to be surprised she had someone with her. Make that a man they'd never met, nor heard of, and they'd be agog with questions.

'Hey, Chloe, how's your day been?' Giuseppe asked when she stepped into the kitchen after tying Genie up.

'Busy as usual. Guys, I want you to meet someone.' She turned to Devlin and, hand on his arm, pulled him into the hot space. 'This is Devlin Walsh. He's an emergency specialist and started in ED last week.'

Lorenzo wiped his hands on his apron and held one out to Devlin. 'Pleased to meet you. I'm Lorenzo. This is my brother, Giuseppe. Are you joining our girl for dinner?'

Our girl. As if she were the pet in this relationship. Chloe laughed. 'Yes, he is.'

'Hello, Devlin.' Giuseppe put his hand out, too, his eyes firmly fixed on Dev.

Looking for what? Chloe wondered. Deciding if he was good enough for her, as any decent brothers would?

Devlin shook hands all round. 'Nice to meet

you both. This is the first time I've come into a restaurant through the back door.'

It'll be the last time if these two don't take to you, Chloe thought.

Dev must've picked on that, too, as he added, 'Hopefully I pass muster and it won't be the last.'

Giuseppe gave him a long, hard look that many would've turned away from.

Not Devlin. 'I used to know Chloe in Auckland and now we're working together, which is a first.'

Lorenzo, the more accepting of the brothers, grinned. 'Hope you know who's in charge, Devlin. No one gets away with much around our Chloe.'

'Like I said, I used to know her.'

Chloe struggled to take back control before he started telling them how well they'd known each other. 'What's the special tonight, Lorenzo?'

'Wait and see.'

'Same as last week, then.' She laughed, suddenly nervous. It had been a bad idea to agree to come here with Devlin. These guys might be keeping their questions to themselves, but past experience had taught her they wouldn't put them aside for ever. 'We'll go and sit down, get out of your hair.'

'That'd work if I had any.' Finally Giuseppe was smiling his usual broad smile. Dev had obviously passed the first step, whatever that was in Giuseppe's book. 'Come on. I'll pour you both a wine.' He gave Chloe a quick hug. 'How was your holiday? Your *mamma* is all right? And *papà*?'

'They're both good, and send their love to you two and the rest of the family.' Whenever her mother and stepdad came to Wellington they dined here, and visited with the guys' sisters and parents. 'They also said you have to go over and stay when you close for the winter break. Take the tribe with you.'

'We take three weeks and have about six weeks' worth of invitations to use,' Lorenzo called from the kitchen. 'I tell you, Joy and Jack's will be the first stop.'

Placing two glasses on the counter, Giuseppe added, 'Knowing how they will spoil us, it might be the only one. Three weeks lounging around in the Sounds, going boating, fishing, and eating fresh fish is the idyllic holiday.' He turned to the fridge for a bottle of the Chardonnay that Chloe enjoyed.

'Hang on. Devlin prefers a red.'

Giuseppe's eyebrow rose as he looked from her to Devlin. 'That's so?'

Damn, he'd worked out they might know each other better than first indicated.

Dev picked up fast. 'Old habits don't change,' he acknowledged. 'What brands of Pinot Noir do you have?' He leaned closer to the wine rack. 'Is that a South Otago one?' Lifting it out, he read the label and handed the bottle to Giuseppe. 'That one, please.'

'Good taste, I see.' Her 'brother' flicked a quick glance her way, before going back to pouring the wine and studying Dev.

She shouldn't have come here with Devlin. But what choice had she had when he'd asked? She had been tempted to say no, but not a lot in her head, or heart, could manage it. Spending time with him away from work helped cement the fact they were getting along well enough to not bite each other's heads off over any little thing. It was in their DNA to face facts, not avoid them.

But I haven't mentioned the miscarriage.

Not now. Don't even think about it. Don't spoil what was going so well.

Dev picked both wine glasses up and nodded across the room. 'Is that table with the reserved sign yours?'

'Yep. This place will be humming soon.' Half the tables were already full and people were relaxing with wine and delicious food. This was only Wednesday and early, but it was a restaurant locals used regularly. 'Wait until you see this on a Friday evening. Standing room only.'

'As if we let that happen.' Giuseppe grinned. 'Too messy when someone spills their food.'

As she sank onto her chair, Chloe told Devlin, 'The guys prefer catering for locals. More reliable, and getting to know individuals suits their personalities. Plus many folk from the Italian community are regulars. The guys often close it to the public on a Sunday so that family and friends can enjoy themselves as only the Italians know how.'

'We live and work in this area. It's home in all ways.' Lorenzo had come out with a plate of arancini al burro, which he placed on the table. 'Rice balls in batter.'

Devlin sat down. 'How long does it take to become a regular? If you're going to produce food like this I'm booking my own table.' And he hadn't even tasted one.

'You can put your name on Chloe's as long as you look out for her.'

If he didn't, he wouldn't get in the front—or back—door again. Chloe tried not to smile too widely. These guys were her brothers in all ways except genes, and likely as fierce, if not more, than real ones would be. 'Thanks, Lorenzo. Can Devlin have a menu? He doesn't know what you create yet.'

'Here.' Giuseppe flourished a folder. 'Take your time. But everything is delicious.'

Finally they were left to themselves, and Chloe felt her muscles start to relax. 'Sorry about that. They can be full on, but I wouldn't change them for anything.'

'A couple of characters, for sure.' Dev studied her as he sipped his wine. 'I like that you've got friends like them. Everyone needs someone to fall back on at times.'

'Who said I've ever done that with them?'

'There's a sense of comfort and safety that touches you whenever you talk to them. What happened?'

Great. Walked into that one without even realising. She'd forgotten how well Dev could read her. But after all these years, she'd thought he'd have lost that skill with her at least. 'It's not important.'

Devlin sat back and waited. He knew she wouldn't be able to remain quiet for ever. She didn't used to be able to anyway. Then again, she'd toughened up lately. Hadn't she?

'There was a man.'

His face tightened.

'He was a regular here. Used to sit in the corner at the back, always on his own. He'd eat spaghetti bolognese every night, drink one glass of prosecco, and walk out after paying cash. Until…' She paused, took a mouthful of Chardonnay. It could still make her shiver when she thought of him. 'One night he seemed to take an inordinate amount of notice of me. He never spoke to me, or acknowledged me, just watched me while he ate and drank.'

'How long did that go on for?' There was a fierce, angry thread in Dev's voice.

'I only come in here once or twice a week, but he continued for a month.' More wine spilled over her dry tongue. 'Then one night he waited outside and started to follow me home. It was winter and dark but I knew he was there, so I did an about-turn and returned here. Lorenzo drove me home, I talked to the police but there was nothing they could do as he hadn't approached me, let alone anything else.'

'What happened?' Dev ground out.

'I never saw him again. He's never been in here since. All the guys will say is that Giuseppe had a word with him and he agreed to find somewhere else to eat. They also talked to the cops, and word has it the man left town shortly afterwards. I don't know anything else, and no one's saying a thing. But the Italian community have a reputation for looking out for their own.'

'He lives in another town and won't be returning to Wellington any time soon,' Giuseppe said as he went past with a tray of drinks for a table at the front.

'But you never decided to leave the city yourself,' Devlin said. 'I'm impressed. Not that you were ever a gutless wonder, but you always did like to feel safe.'

'I still do, only on my terms now.' Hell, she'd told Devlin more about herself than anyone else in the last seven years. But then, he'd always been easy to talk with, and had a way about him that prompted confidence.

'I'm glad the guys were here for you.' The tightness in his voice told her he'd have done the same had he been around when it happened.

'So am I. Can we talk about something else? It gives me the creeps even thinking about that man. Did you sell your Auckland home before coming south?' If he had it would mean he wasn't in a rush to return to the family, and they must be freaking out that he'd gone. Number one favourite son was meant to be there for all the society events.

'No, it's rented out, but not just as a backstop in case I change my mind over living here. This is a permanent move.'

'Sticking to your guns might not be easy.'

'You have no idea.' Then he really looked at her. 'Wrong. Of course you do.'

Bam. His parents were between them again. 'I wasn't what they'd envisaged as their daughter-in-law and, if I was going to say anything in their favour, I wasn't exactly the right type for all that socialising and being glammed up. I get that. I tried so hard to be more like your mother wished, but it wasn't in me to put having my nails done before putting my hand up for an extra shift at the hospital. I own that.'

A large, warm hand covered hers. 'I'm sorry. I did talk to them about it whenever it got too bad, but I thought you'd want to fight your own battles. You were always saying how much you fought with Joy as a kid. Maybe I should have tried harder, said more.'

She didn't want to move away from that touch. Not at all. The warmth and gentle strength in his fingers and palms reminded her of too many wonderful times with Devlin, of reliance and trust and love. Which was why she slid her hand away and picked up her glass again. There hadn't been much of that in the last days of their relationship. Though he had just admitted he could have done more for her, but the blame wasn't all his. She could have talked to him about it.

'I did, and I also wanted to know you were right behind me. I was a bit of a scrapper growing up. Any kid with only one parent and living in poverty was. It was how we survived. But the day I started training to become a nurse I vowed never to be like that again.'

'Except it's in your veins. That attitude saved you time and again from put-downs and other people's venom. I saw you react when someone was rude to you in an emergency department or on a ward. You'd lift your shoulders and chin, and glare at them to say, "Don't mess with me. Ever."' He smiled.

'So Wellington's the real deal?'

He laughed. 'Persistent, aren't you? Yes, it is. I don't intend returning to Auckland, at least until I've given this opportunity a real chance.' He was looking over her shoulder to the far wall. 'Auckland's the only place I've lived, and I want to expand my horizons, find where I'd like to be.'

This from the man who'd warned her when he'd proposed that he'd never leave Auckland permanently, that his family came first over everything. 'You're serious.'

His eyes returned to her. 'Yes, Chloe, I am.'

What had happened to change him? He was different. For one, he'd never have admitted what he'd just told her. He'd liked to appear in control of himself if nothing else, even when it was obvious his parents had a hold over him—a hold called *family*. They were his family, not hers, and even if their marriage had gone ahead she'd always have come second in their eyes. 'Tell me more.' Would he? Wouldn't he?

She nibbled one of the deep-fried balls as she waited. Better than nibbling her fingernail. Did this move have anything to do with their break up, as long ago as it was? More pressure from his parents because of what she'd supposedly done? The muscles in her legs tightened. Why this fascination about what'd been going on in Devlin's life since they'd split?

'I never really settled once you'd gone.' He blinked, as though he'd gone too far.

She wasn't suggesting he stopped. This was so unlike the Devlin of old who never admitted to having any difficulties in his private life. She picked up another ball and nibbled at it, trying to ignore the tension in her body, the dryness making eating difficult.

'Something was missing. I know we were finished, yet it took some getting used to being alone again.'

'You could've talked to me.' As she'd begged so often.

'I see that now.' He stopped, sipped his wine, continued. 'Work was fine. In fact, it became my regular go-to place most of the time.'

'It always was,' she said without hesitation.

Then blushed when he studied her. 'It's true. I lost count of the number of times you'd forget we had a date and I'd learn you were working extra hours.' She'd resented that at times, even knowing he'd had to put in as much time as possible to qualify. He just hadn't seemed to have an off switch.

'Is that why you went out with your friends so much?'

If that was a loaded question, then he'd get an honest answer. 'Yes. I understood you had to put in the hours but occasionally I wanted to let my hair down—with you. I understood you weren't as free as me, your study took up more time than mine, but for you not to turn up for our dates hurt, so eventually I gave up sitting around in my flat and went out with my girlfriends.' She had to put it out there one last time. 'I did not ever cheat on you.'

Pushing his plate aside, Devlin reached for her hands, holding them tight. 'I think I know that.' He shook his head. 'No, I do know that. Now. Since I saw you on Monday in ED I just knew I'd badly messed up. I keep replaying that night, trying to see it from your perspective. You were shocked, angry and hurt. It's the anger that's woken me up to the truth. You were furious because I wouldn't hear you out.'

'You never once gave me the benefit of doubt. It was your way or no way.'

'You're right. I was so convinced you'd done the same thing as Cath, I didn't want to hear your excuses. I deleted your text messages without reading them and blocked your number, then threw away all the notes you left in the letterbox. I'm so sorry.' Sadness filled his eyes.

She was stunned. Now what? Reaching for her glass, she took a big gulp. It did nothing to change the shock souring her mouth. They wouldn't have had to go through all the pain of their break up if he'd thought this through years ago. But he hadn't, and they had broken up. Nothing could change that. So... Another gulp of wine, and the glass was empty. 'I'm glad you've finally accepted the truth, albeit seven years on.' The glass spun in her fingers. 'Now we have to move on as colleagues and maybe eventually friends.'

The sadness etched his face. 'Of course.'

'Dev, I—'

'Here you go, lovely. Main course.' Giovanni placed dishes of bubbling lasagne before each of them. 'I'll get you another glass of Chardonnay.'

Lovely. That was Giuseppe being protective, telling her he and Lorenzo were watching out for her. Had he overheard their conversation?

Had he deliberately interrupted her before she said too much, put her heart on the line without thinking it through? Because she did care for Dev. Far too much. Him acknowledging his mistake had her letting go of the knots of anger and hurt she hadn't realised she still carried.

Chloe shook her head. 'My hips' favourite.'

'Like there's a problem.' Devlin laughed. 'You're never going to win the award for being overweight.'

True. She had lean genes. 'I'm lucky. But sometimes I probably test the boundaries a little bit too much.' It went back to her insecurities growing up and also how Stephen had always told her she was fat when she'd been almost skinny. 'Hard to resist food like this though.' She had finally accepted herself for who she was, and to hell with what anyone else thought. Mostly, anyway.

'I mightn't be so lucky.' Devlin forked up a mouthful, chewed, smiled with more exuberance. 'It's going to be hard to stay away from here.'

There went her quiet go-to restaurant. She'd always be on the lookout for him and, depending on how her day had gone if they were on the same shift, she'd be happy or not so pleased to see him. 'Did you know I was living in Wellington before you moved here?'

'Hardly. I heard you'd moved south, but you could've been anywhere by now.'

'I guess I could have.' But she was here in Wellington, where Devlin had recently decided to make a permanent life. 'Where's that wine, Giuseppe?'

CHAPTER FIVE

'I'LL WALK YOU HOME,' Dev said as Chloe untied Genie outside the restaurant.

'No need. We do it all the time.' It wasn't far, the streets were well lit, and Chloe doubted she could take much more of his company without saying something she'd later regret. Like how great it would be to spend more time alone with him. Because she was seeing the man she'd first fallen for, only older and more interesting. He was calmer and more at ease with himself, something he hadn't been before.

'Not on my watch, you don't.'

'Don't forget Nonna's lunch on Sunday.' Lorenzo was standing in the doorway, arms folded across his chest.

Bet he'd heard Dev saying he'd see her home. The questions would be firing at lunch come Sunday. 'As if I'd forget her birthday.' She crossed the deck and gave Lorenzo a hug, whispering, 'Don't even think about quizzing me.'

He gave her a tighter than usual hug, said quietly, 'Bring him with you to the party, if you like.'

'I don't think so.' It was too soon, if indeed there was ever going to be a time she'd introduce Devlin to her other family. 'Catch you Sunday.'

'Nice meeting you, Devlin,' Lorenzo said over the top of her head as she pulled away.

'Likewise. I'll be back for another meal soon.'

'Good.'

Chloe stepped off the porch, Genie at her knee. Time to get home and relax. Not that she hadn't been relaxed over dinner, but there'd been this feeling that any moment now Dev was going to start asking about whether she had a man in her life, or who she'd been dating since they split up and if she was on her own, why. She wasn't ready to talk about the drought that was her love life. She'd have to admit she'd been unaware until she'd seen him again that she hadn't got over him, and, as she was still getting her head around that, she didn't really have any answers she was willing to share.

'I wouldn't be surprised if one of those guys doesn't follow us just to make sure I behave like a gentleman.' Devlin laughed. 'They really have your back, don't they?'

'You'd better believe it.' She joined in the laughter, but it was true. Both men had taken her under their wing right from that day she'd helped Lorenzo with his burns. Almost as though they'd seen past her barriers to the woman inside and the hurt she'd carried, and how she didn't trust men with her heart, unless they only wanted to be friends. 'I found me a family without trying.'

'I bet you give back as much as or more than they do.'

'No comment.' She smiled, and stretched out her steps. It was colder now and a hot shower and a cup of tea in front of the fire was tempting. As was a break from this sexy man matching her strides.

They reached her front gate in what felt like record time, and Chloe bit her tongue, trying not to invite Devlin in for a hot drink. It felt natural, but if she did she wondered if she'd be able to resist hugging him, maybe even kissing him. Her body ached to do so, to feel his warmth under her palms, know the movement of his muscles again. But for once her head was winning the battle and keeping her hormones in control. Barely, but barely was enough.

'Thanks for seeing us home,' she said as she unlatched the gate.

He was looking beyond her. 'You've got

yourself a tidy little cottage, Looks like you've had the outside repainted fairly recently.'

Pride inflated her chest. 'I did it myself last summer. At first it was daunting, but the further along I got the more I found I enjoyed the prep and then the painting. The result was beyond what I had hoped for.'

'You continue to surprise me, Chloe Rasmussen. Is this your for ever home? Or is it an investment?'

'At the moment, it's my for ever place. I love living here, in *my* house, making changes as I see fit.' But hopefully one day she would settle down with the man of her dreams and make the move into another property. That dream had never been completely discarded, just the bit about who it might include. 'It's small—the second bedroom can barely fit a single bed. At the moment it's my sewing room.'

'Sewing room? As in making clothes? Or curtains for the house?' He looked stunned.

But then she hadn't known how to use a sewing machine back in the days they were together. Another thing she owed her trip to Italy for. Milan and fashion were Brigitta's passion and it had rubbed off on her, though she still didn't dress up as often as she should. Had to have somewhere to go for that. 'Dresses, coats, trousers. You name it. I can make them.' A wedding dress. Air hissed over her teeth.

Wrong, Chloe. So wrong to be thinking that.

Tell that to her heart when she was standing next to Devlin, who looked so delicious she wanted to eat him. Taste him, kiss him, touch his shoulders, back, everywhere.

He was staring at her as though for the very first time and seemed to be seeing something that fascinated him. And stirred his blood because there was something akin to lust filling his eyes. 'Chloe…' The tip of his tongue appeared between his lips.

Her pulse quickened. Her upper body leaned towards him.

Don't, Chloe. It's too soon.

But those eyes were dragging her in. The face she'd once fallen in love with was so close. She could almost feel her palm touching his chin, his cheek, her lips kissing his.

No, Chloe. Not now. Not yet.

Deep breath.

'Chloe.' Dev sighed her name as though on a breeze.

Her arms lifted, lay over his shoulders, around his neck, ever so gently pulling them together. 'Dev.'

Their lips met, carefully, tenderly. Opened under each other, pressed harder, closer.

Their tongues clashed, pulled back, moved forward again.

Chloe melted into Dev's solid body, absorbing his heat and strength and gentleness as her mouth brought more deliciousness to her starved heart. 'Dev.'

He held her tight yet softly, his hands on her backside, his thighs and belly and chest against hers, his mouth devouring her. Magic swirled in the air around them, encasing them in their own world.

Thud. Something solid banged the back of her knee.

What? Oh, it was Genie.

Devlin dropped his arms, stepped back.

Chloe blinked, looking from Dev to the dog and back to Dev. She'd kissed him. And loved feeling him against her, his mouth on hers. Loved it. What had she done? 'Goodnight,' she muttered and raced up the path to her front door, denying herself the opportunity to turn around and drink in more of those good looks and that stunning body.

Chloe slid into bed and switched the light off. Even in the total blackness, she saw Devlin's face in her mind.

'Dev.' His name whispered across her lips.

The tip of her tongue traced her lips where his had been. 'Devlin.'

She shuffled down the mattress to lie on her back, staring up where the ceiling was, and a rough sigh spilled out. Followed by another. Longer, rougher, sad. Squeezing her eyes shut tight, she focused on the image of that strong face, blue eyes, and sexy mouth that had delivered the sweetest of kisses. And the most demanding ones. Kisses that turned her on in a blink.

Her eyes shot open. Yes. Devlin had turned her into a molten blob of heat and longing within an instant. Nothing new there, she'd thought. But actually there was. They were different people now. So many years spent doing different things. Of course, they'd changed. Yet there was a familiarity at being in his arms, kissing that sensuous mouth, that she couldn't deny. It had just gripped her. Could they really do this? Rewrite their past?

Staring around, she picked out the shape of her dressing table, the doorframe, in the weak light from the street lights now shoving that total darkness aside. The familiarity did nothing to quieten her thudding head—and heart. Devlin had once owned her heart. But she needed to slow down right now. One kiss at a time. Not rush in without looking around this time, or they'd be back to square one all too soon.

He'd turned her world upside down just by being himself. He might have changed but he still had the power to blindside her with softness and heat and need and annoyance. By talking to her, looking at her, touching her elbow when she tripped over a rough patch on the footpath as they'd walked home.

Damn you, Devlin. Couldn't you have stayed away for ever? Chosen another city to put your feet down in? Left me to the quiet, comfortable life I've finally made for myself?

After only three days everything had changed, and nothing would be the same again. She was already back to square one. A different square, but just as confusing.

He was the man she'd given her heart to, fallen for so deeply it had been hard to find herself afterwards, and when she had, she'd vowed she'd never give her heart or soul away again. Dev had supported her when she'd struggled with training to be a nurse, he'd been beside her when she'd qualified, had talked about how many kids they might have one day, where they'd live, who'd be the best cook and worst gardener. He'd been everything to her.

Too much, maybe? Had she taken more than she'd given? Had she relied on him too much to find her feet in an adult world where she was supposed to be in charge of her own destiny while always looking for the sky to fall in on her? A habit learned as a child when her mother had kept them on the move as she'd tried to find her own place in the world. People had come and gone throughout those early years, teachers, friends, and neighbours. While her mother had always been her rock, the time had come when she'd had to make her own way, and she'd met Stephen after leaving school and doing her pre-nursing studies. She'd probably moved in with him too quickly, but it had felt right at the time. She'd needed to be loved. Got that wrong big time. She had found the courage to leave him and thought that was it for love for a while, then along had come Devlin with his solidness, reliability, and devastating kisses, and her world had finally stopped rolling and settled. He was her match in every way. Or so she'd thought.

Wrong, Chloe. Oh, so wrong.

Except he had just apologised for hurting her, had owned his error. A lone tear trickled from the corner of her eye down the side of her face into her ear. Then another. And another.

Slapping them away, she continued staring at the ceiling. Nothing there to distract the upsetting thoughts and memories.

Sitting at the restaurant, enjoying a meal, talking like they used to had sucked her right back in, made her feel comfortable with Devlin, made her feel desirable again. It had been too easy to let the past fall away—as though it had only been a glitch between them. But it hadn't been. Yet for a few hours she'd forgotten everything else and just enjoyed being with him.

Be honest, Chloe. You more than enjoyed his company. You loved it. You might even still love him.

The tears were running fast now. Filling her ears, soaking her hair.

She flipped over and buried her face in the pillow, her hand a fist in her mouth to prevent the raw pain exploding out. Her chest was aching from the beating it was getting. The tears were a torrent as a sob tore out of her. She couldn't love Devlin. Hadn't for a while. She'd put him aside, moved on.

Put him aside only to pick up again when he'd turned up in her life?

'No.' The denial groaned across her lips.

So why the familiar pain? The old sense of wonder whenever he was near? Why did she feel more relaxed around Devlin than she'd been with anyone else in the intervening years?

This was plain crazy. She could not love Devlin.

Something solid nudged her arm.

'Genie?'

You weren't thinking Devlin had turned up, were you?

Nudge. Bump. Bang. Genie sprawled alongside her.

Chloe rolled onto her side and reached out to stroke her pet's head, sniffing at her tears. 'Hey, my girl.' More tears spilled down her face. Damn it. *This* was love. Simple, filled with warmth and food and shelter. No complications. No accusations that not any amount of denials got rid of.

Damn it. None of this was keeping Devlin out of her mind. He was back in full force. Just like old times.

Except nothing was like their relationship back then. Now they worked together. She owned a house. She was stronger, believed in herself and didn't need to be boosted into believing she was good enough for him. That one fault in particular had caused a lot of problems in the past. Now she knew better. If someone didn't like her or the way she went about things, then that was their problem, not hers.

Genie pushed closer.

'That's enough, my girl. I do have to get some sleep.'

Another day, another shift working alongside Devlin. Her new reality. One that had her in a state of uncertainty. Except working with Delvin was fine. That kiss was tipping her off track. With it came that special bond they'd shared over most aspects of their lives. It had also brought home how good they were together. *And* how she'd like to feel that again.

She would? Of course she would. She didn't want to spend the rest of her life single, or without children. But she hadn't done very well finding another man she'd even consider getting close to and possibly settling down for the long haul with. They weren't exactly lining up for her to take notice. Then along came Dev once more and suddenly her heart was beating more erratically than it had done in years, and she just plain felt more at ease and ready for an adventure than she had in for ever. Devlin. Was this all down to his reappearance in her life?

What other reason could there be? Nothing was popping up in her head. Her hands fisted on either side of her thighs. 'Damn it. Damn you, Devlin. Why, why, why did you come to Wellington? Now I have to deal with these feelings that are marching through me like an unstoppable parade.'

Genie dropped her head on Chloe's shoulder. 'Sorry, girl. I don't know what's come over me. I'm beginning to think I might still love

Devlin. Not in an "old boyfriend who could now be a friend" kind of way, but in a complete, heart-rending, body-warming, mind-blowing way.' As she used to.

Thump, thump, thump. Her nails poked into her palms. The bed shook. What had she done? Nothing. The question should be, did she want to love Devlin again? No, she didn't. He'd accused her of cheating on him, and then refused to listen to her replies. Why would she want to love him?

Because he was the only man to ever light her fires so hot, so big, so wonderfully. That she could start reacting to him so strongly as soon as she'd seen him again had to have been a warning that all was not how she'd thought it should be, that she hadn't yet reached the point where she was truly over him. Spending the evening with him at the restaurant had only enhanced all those feelings a hundred times over, ringing giant warning bells.

What was she going to do? Leap in and see what happened? Devlin would be out of town within seconds.

Then go for it. Make him aware of you in other ways than as a nurse in the same department.

They'd already started that process over dinner, so keep up the momentum. No, there'd only be one loser and she wasn't ready to go through all that heartache again. She'd have to continue being professional at work and stay away from dinner dates or walks on the beach except with Genie.

Tossing the sheet aside, she swung her legs over the side of the bed and stood up. This was not working. She needed sleep, not nightmares—or dreams that were never going to be realised. So she'd settle for a hot chocolate drink sitting on the couch with the curtains open so she could gaze up at the stars until her pulse slowed to normal and her head stopped spinning.

Dressed in jeans and a merino jersey, Devlin sat on his deck, his feet propped on the top of the glass balustrade, a glass with a shot of malt whisky in his hand. He should be in bed sleeping the sleep of the dead. His body ached with exhaustion, but his mind was wide awake and busy.

The weeks leading to arriving in Wellington and unpacking his household belongings and everything else he'd managed to accumulate over the years had been intense. Meeting new colleagues and learning the ropes of the department had kept him on his toes, and happy, and reminding himself this was what *he* wanted. But it was Chloe who'd thrown his calm to the wind.

From that first moment when he'd seen her dealing with the patient who'd had a cardiac arrest he'd known deep down he was in trouble. Like a ticking time bomb inside him, his body tensed on and off with regular distractions, and his head kept spinning left and right. If he still believed he could work with Chloe and not get sidetracked, then he was screwed. The last thing he wanted to be was continually distracted. It made concentrating on patients difficult. No, that wasn't true. Every time he and Chloe worked together with a patient, he was completely focused on what he was meant to be doing. It was only when they paused, or moved on to another patient, that his mind started playing games with him.

They'd kissed tonight. He'd been drawn straight back to the very first time he'd kissed her and the sense of having found his love, his better half. Tonight had been no different. They belonged together. Or at least they had. Chloe in his arms as he kissed her, her slight body wrapped around him as they made love, her tinkling laughter when they shared a funny moment. Sadness and pain in her eyes when they argued. Yes, those emotions were there every day as they worked together, when they walked on the beach. Like memories overlaid with new yet similar images. Where did this take him? Take them? Since the day he'd broken off their engagement he'd refused to think about Chloe and what he'd lost. What was the point in regrets?

Now that kiss showed he hadn't got over her. She was still in his system. Still capable of making him breathe faster. Still giving him a reason to smile. Twisting his belly whenever he looked at her. Making his heart thump.

The whisky slid over his tongue and down his throat, warming him as it went.

Chloe had told him the truth. Believing his mother had proved to be the wrong decision but had she genuinely been misled, too, and believed she'd acted in his best interests? Or had she deliberately tried to cause problems for him and Chloe? No, he still couldn't believe she'd go that far and deliberately break his heart just to get her own way with him. She must have known there was only so far he could be pushed before he pushed back. He'd left Auckland to get away from his parents interfering in his life, trying to suggest he marry someone of their choice who didn't tick his boxes.

Tick his boxes? Try tighten his belly into tiny knots of desire and heat and need.

Wiping his hand over his face in a vague attempt to hold the exhaustion at bay, he laughed mirthlessly at himself. Chloe Rasmussen had waltzed right back into his head—and his body—and there was no getting away from her. Not even out here, fifteen floors up, in the cool night air where no one could see him. He was alone, and yet he wasn't. She was always with him. That was how he'd used to feel when they were a couple. Chloe was always there for him, and in his soul when they weren't together in the same room.

She should not be with him now.

They were long finished as a couple.

Weren't they? Their kiss said otherwise. Kissing Chloe had made him feel as though he'd come home. The woman he'd once accused of having an affair. Shame gnawed at him, felt ghastly. How could he have made such an awful error of judgement and wrecked what should've been a wonderful future with the woman of his dreams?

Chloe had been all of that, and more. He'd loved her so much. Had his ego got in the way? The whisky soothed his throat but not his mind. Three days working with her, and then going out for a meal followed by that sensational kiss, and he couldn't deny he still had feelings for her. Old ones that he hadn't managed to get over after all. Like how his body went soft with longing whenever she walked into the room. How his heart tripped when she touched him. The way she slept with one hand under her cheek and the other on his chest.

Could they start over? Was he falling for Chloe as fast and deep as before? No, he wasn't falling in love with her again. Because he hadn't stopped loving her in the first place. Had he? Of course, he had, he must have. Hell. This was getting completely out of hand. He didn't know what he thought or how he felt.

Devlin jumped to his feet, drained his glass and strode inside, closing the glass door behind him. If he was going to sit out there having these dim-witted ideas, then he might as well go to bed and try to get some sleep. He'd swallow some magnesium tablets to help with that.

As he slid between the sheets, one good thought crossed his mind. He would be out of town from Friday till Monday, going up to Auckland to finalise some legal paperwork surrounding his properties and attending his cousin's wedding on a vineyard west of the city. There'd be little or no time to spend thinking about Chloe. He'd have a break from her and hopefully calm down.

Just had to get through tomorrow first. And put aside the warm sensations that kiss had brought to his body and heart.

* * *

Chloe had the wipers on full speed and still had to peer through the windscreen to see clearly. It was bucketing down and the wind was driving the rain sideways. Parking and making a dash along the street to the hospital had her wondering if calling in sick might've been a good idea. At least she'd have been warm and dry. As if she'd do that, she thought with a sigh.

'Welcome to windy Wellington,' she said to Devlin a quarter of an hour later as they both entered the ED hub at the same time, her hands itching to touch him again.

'Who'd want to be on a ferry this morning?' he agreed politely.

'Not me, that's for sure.' The Interislander ferries running between Picton and Wellington often had high winds and huge swells, and it was not fun to be on board at those times. 'Far prefer it when it's perfectly flat. Which is very rare on the Cook Strait.' Pulling up a chair, she sat down and brought up the screen to go through last night's patient list and focus on anything but Dev. 'What've we got, Jaz?'

'It was a busy night. Two car crashes, a policeman shot in the arm, and one five-year-old with RSV.' Jaz stretched, hands rubbing the small of her back. 'I hope that's not the beginning of more to come.'

'It's a fast-acting virus, highly contagious, especially amongst youngsters, so I expect to see more cases in the coming weeks,' Devlin commented.

'Throw in this being the middle of winter,' Chloe muttered.

'Agreed.' Devlin was reading a file on the computer next to her. 'Let's hope it doesn't get out of hand.'

A yawn gripped her. Beside her Dev was doing the same, and she couldn't hold back a laugh. 'You, too?'

'Yes,' he muttered.

'Morning, everyone.'

Chloe glanced up and around, surprised to find the space filled with the day-shift staff. She hadn't been aware of anyone other than Dev and Jaz. 'Hi, Clare. Busy night by the looks of it.'

'It was. Jaz, get out of here while you can. Everyone else's gone.' Clare got down to business. 'Devlin, everyone, you've got a woman in cubicle ten, admitted at four with severe abdomen pain. Suspected kidney stone. We're waiting on blood results and the urologist is due in before seven. A forty-five-year-old male, suspected mild stroke during the night, no known history. I've given him blood thinners, and we're keeping him in under observation for a few hours.'

The list went on and Chloe divvied up the patients between the other nurses. 'I'll take triage,' she told them at the end of Clare's outline. That'd keep her out of the main area and away from Devlin most of the time. All part of downplaying her reactions to him, and staying sane for the day.

She needn't have worried about getting too close to him. The day was manic with a steady stream of patients coming through the front door by foot or through the ambulance bay on a bed. At two o'clock she got a call from the head nurse, Sandy. 'Hi, Chloe. Busy day, I hear.'

Chloe sighed. She knew what was coming. 'Who's not turning up for the next shift?'

'Shayne. He's come down with a stomach bug. You up for it?'

She was hardly going to say no, even when she was shattered. 'It's why you ring me first. You know I hardly ever say no.'

Sandy sounded a little embarrassed when she said, 'Sorry. I was panicking a bit. Had another no show yesterday and I still don't know if she'll be in or not today. Take a break, have some coffee and a snack, go for a brisk walk before you start the next shift.'

'It's stopped raining?' It had still been hosing down last time she'd been in triage and had looked out of the front doors.

'Drizzling now. You shouldn't get too wet.'

'Gee, Sandy, you're a cheer.' But a walk might do wonders for her tired body. 'I'll go across the road for a decent coffee and a slice of quiche.'

'Don't let the cafeteria staff hear you say that. They think their coffee's the best.'

It was hospital grade, a standard joke amongst the staff, who drank gallons of coffee twenty-four-seven. 'They'd lynch me, I know. Okay, I'm up for it. I'm not even going to mention hoping that we have a quiet evening.' She'd done that too often with crazy consequences.

At the far side of the hub Devlin was typing up notes. 'You staying on?'

'Yep. I'm about to take an hour's break first.' It was routine when someone carried on through the next shift.

'What about Genie? Won't she need feeding and a walk?'

'I'll phone my neighbour when she gets home from school. She takes care of Genie for me when I'm on afternoon and evening shifts.' Then Chloe recalled something. 'Damn, that won't work.'

'Problem?' Devlin had swung around on his chair and was watching her.

'Just remembered Zoe is away on a school trip.'

'I'll drop by and take her to the beach for a walk. Feed her as well.'

'You don't have to do that. I can call somebody else.' Devlin was offering to help her out. He couldn't have any hang ups about last night, then.

'I know I don't, but I'd like to. It'll get me moving, instead of sitting around my apartment with little to do.' One side of his mouth lifted in a wry smile. 'Pathetic, eh?'

'Fine, thanks. Genie'll think you're wonderful, and be beholden to you. There's food in the fridge and biscuits in the pantry. There's a spare key on a nail just inside her kennel.'

Genie would probably take it off the hook and give it to Dev. She could be fickle in her affections when it came to getting walks and food.

'Consider it done.' He stood up and stretched that long body she used to know far too well.

Still did, if her memory of muscular abs and firm buttocks was anything to go by. Then there was the way her arms had wound around him last night. As if they hadn't taken a seven-year break. Quiet, girl. He was about to go off shift, and she had another eight hours to see through. There wasn't any energy to spare for even thinking about his body. Tell that to someone who'd believe her. She could always drum up the energy to think about Dev's body. 'Thanks. I'll see you next week.' Hadn't he mentioned going north for the weekend? Maybe he'd get back sooner than expected and drop by for a coffee. Or even another kiss?

CHAPTER SIX

'HOW WAS YOUR WEEKEND?' Chloe asked on Monday morning as Dev strolled in to begin the shift looking far too sexy in the drab blue scrubs. She hadn't seen him since last Thursday, but she had dreamed about him far too often. 'Oh, Genie says hi.'

'She's a right little con. I'm sure I fed her far too much.'

'One nudge and lots of wagging wins her most things she wants,' Chloe agreed, trying not to ogle him.

'I was in Auckland. Had a family wedding to go to as well as a few things to finalise. How was yours?'

'Quiet. Went to the guys' grandmother's birthday lunch at the restaurant on Sunday, and it was fantastic. Also went downtown to a couple of bars with friends on Saturday. That was it.' Nothing too exciting, no hot man in sight.

'I went to a winery in Masterton for lunch,'

Jaz piped up. 'Had the best steak I've ever had. The wine was amazing, too.'

Chloe crossed over to give her a hug. 'Happy birthday, girlfriend. I hope Toby spoiled you.'

Jaz blushed and held out her hand. 'I'd say so.'

'Wow. Would you look at that?' She took Jaz's hand in hers to gaze at the sparkling diamonds. 'That's beautiful. Congratulations. This deserves another hug.'

Jaz grinned, and sniffed. 'I'm still pinching myself.'

Chloe sniffed too. 'You two are destined to be together. Decided on a date yet?'

I am not jealous. Much.

Oh, to be planning a wedding and dreaming of a future with the man of her heart.

'February. If I can wait that long.'

'Time will fly. There's so much to do arranging a wedding.' Not that she'd had a lot of experience. Hers had been pretty much taken over by Mrs Walsh because Chloe had been told she just wouldn't have got it right.

'We're going for small and casual. I think.' Jaz was gazing at her ring with awe in her eyes. 'There again...'

'Can I add my congratulations, too?' Devlin stepped up.

'Everyone's welcome.' Jaz grinned.

Chloe returned to her computer, her heart pounding dully. A wedding. Phew. She'd wanted a cream, off-the-shoulder, tight-fitting gown that flared over her hips to fall to the floor. Daffodils for the bouquet. Her hair falling in long curls over her shoulders, the way Dev liked it.

The pen she'd picked up slid from her lifeless fingers.

'Here.' Devlin picked up the pen. 'You all right?'

'Why wouldn't I be?' Her eyes slid upward, drank in the strapping specimen standing beside her. Yeah, well, dreams were all a load of hot air. And getting back together with Devlin was completely airy. A fantasy—with no happy ending. Hadn't she told herself she wasn't following through on the feelings she appeared to still be having for him? Their kiss had a lot to answer for, she thought morosely, knocking her carefully held together ideas to bits like this when she should be guarding her heart with everything that was in her. 'I'm good to go. Bring on the shift.' Hopefully it would be busy and there'd be no spare time for watching Devlin and reminiscing about things best forgotten.

'Devlin, we've got a cyclist who was knocked off his bike by a bus,' Cass, the triage nurse, was leading the ambulance paramedic into the department. 'GCS eight, fractures in both legs, pelvis out of alignment.'

'Take him, or her, to Resus. Chloe, where are you today?' Devlin asked.

'Resus one.'

'Right, Cass, Resus one. Tell me what we know about our patient.' He nodded at a paramedic.

Chloe raced to Resus, putting all thoughts of Devlin aside.

The paramedic was telling them, 'Male, thirty-one, James Schultz, banker, and that's it. The police got scant details from his backpack. They're following up with the banks and will be in here soon.'

'According to the receptionist there's no information on a James Schultz in the hospital data,' Cass said.

'Great,' Devlin muttered so only Chloe could hear. 'Let's hope there are no illnesses that could impact on what we have to do here.'

Chloe joined everyone to transfer the man across to the bed from the ambulance trolley. 'He's probably fit if he's a cyclist.' Though that wasn't always the case, it was more often than not. She began swapping out the ambulance leads for the hospital ones to keep track of the man's heart and BP on their equipment.

'James, I'm Devlin, a doctor in the emergency department you've been brought into. Can you hear me?'

One eye opened, sliding shut almost instantly.

'Good. You've been in a serious accident. I'm going to give you some drugs for the pain now, and then we have to assess you for all your injuries.' Devlin looked over to Chloe. 'We'll go with intravenous morphine first.'

'I'll get it. Anything else?'

'Not yet.' He was running his hands over James's skull, his fingers gently searching for soft patches that would indicate a head injury. 'Tell Amy to join us, too. She can observe and learn.'

Amy was the junior doctor on their shift. Chloe nodded. 'And another nurse.' They were going to be busy with this man.

Returning with the drug Devlin had requested, she ran it past Amy to check the expiry date and name of drug, then began inserting a cannula in the back of James's hand.

'Skull indent left side,' Devlin intoned. 'No apparent spinal damage, reacting to stimulus on feet.'

Amy watched every move Devlin made. 'His heart rate's low. Internal bleeding?'

'More than likely. That head wound's not causing too much blood loss. There're no obvious external injuries. He could've taken a handlebar in the gut area, which might've damaged the spleen or liver.' Devlin's fingers were now probing James's abdominal region. 'Swelling above the intestine. Feel that, Amy.' He stepped back to allow the trainee in. 'Chloe, can you phone Theatre and let them know we've got a patient who's going to need urgent surgery? Those leg fractures are a go, and the skull needs pressure released. I'll phone the on-duty orthopaedic surgeon and Radiology. Probably going to need a general surgeon, too, if that abdominal swelling proves there's a damaged organ.'

Reading the monitor before her, Chloe said, 'No changes here. One plus in his favour at least. I'll go make that call.'

Cass poked her head around the curtain. 'James has no known medical problems and is a competitive cyclist.'

Not for a while, he wasn't. Chloe's heart squeezed for the man. Being fit would help his recovery but it wasn't going to save him from months of pain and learning to use his legs again. If he got that lucky. Picking up a phone, she pressed the number for Theatre. 'Hello, Damien. Chloe from ED. We've got a multi-trauma case that's going to need surgery after

X-rays and as soon as the orthopaedic surgeon sees him.'

'We've got a full house this morning. Let me see who I'm going to put back. Okay, there we go. Let the surgeon know we've got a bed in an hour or a bit less. I'm presuming you'll be that long anyway, by the time Radiology, the surgeon and the anaesthetist have done their jobs?'

'Sounds about right. There might be a general surgeon as well as the man is still being assessed for internal injuries.'

'So I need to swap out another op as well. Okay, onto it. Keep us posted.' Damien hung up.

'Theatre's sorted,' she told Devlin, who was sitting at the next desk talking to what sounded like the surgeon.

He gave her a quick nod, mouthed, 'Can you phone Radiology and the porters?'

'Sure.' She picked up the phone again, pressed another button. 'Hi there. Chloe from ED.'

After the calls she headed back to their patient where Devlin was again trying to get a verbal response from him.

'James, this is Devlin. Squeeze my hand if you can hear me. Good. Okay, now we're going to get you X-rayed and a surgeon is also coming to see you.'

'Do we want bloods for a cross match?' Chloe asked.

'Yes.'

'Dianna, can you get the blood kit?' she asked the other nurse. 'And wipes to start cleaning his arms and torso.'

'No problem.' Dianna opened a cupboard on the far wall.

The orthopaedic surgeon arrived, and the room began to feel crowded. But no one was surplus to requirements; they all had a job and were getting on with it quietly and efficiently.

As Chloe took the blood sample she listened to Devlin explaining to the surgeon what little they knew about the patient's injuries. Then as suddenly as James had arrived he was whisked off to Radiology and from there he'd be taken to Theatre and prepared for at least one operation. 'It's going to be a long morning for him,' she commented. Not that he'd know much about it.

'Poor blighter,' Dianna said.

'It's going to be a whole lot worse afterwards,' Devlin added. 'I'd say for a bus versus cyclist he might've got off lightly, if I can call those horrific injuries light.'

'Know what you mean,' she agreed. 'He's alive and breathing, and not totally non-compos. But I wouldn't want to be waking up to learn what's happened.'

'I wonder if there's family or a partner to be there for him.'

'Imagine facing that on your own.' She shuddered. 'There wouldn't be anything worse. Actually, that's not true, but it would be right up there.' She couldn't envisage not having someone special at her side if she were going through something like that. But she'd had to go through a miscarriage alone, hadn't she? Her gaze drifted sideways to Devlin before abruptly returning to focus on the job in hand.

Devlin was looking at her with empathy and a gentle smile.

An old anger burst into her head, and she leapt to her feet. How *could* he have believed she'd cheated on him so easily? It mightn't have looked good having Adam in her flat, but Devlin had never given her a chance to explain properly.

He might have apologised now and admitted he was wrong, but the fact remained he had reacted harshly and swiftly, and refused to hear her out, or even bother to read her note about the miscarriage. How could she think she still had feelings for him when he was capable of that? He could do it to her again. Just as quickly the chill evaporated, taking her sudden surge of anger with it, leaving her feeling hollowed out and worried about what lay ahead. More pain? Or something potentially exciting and loving?

Living here seemed to indicate he might have finally told his family he was living the life he chose, not what they expected of him. The only thing wrong with that idea was Devlin was very loyal to his family, and totally understood where his wealthy lifestyle had come from. He'd never walk away from them completely. Not for her, not for anybody. And she'd be best off remembering that.

'Chloe?'

'Yes?'

Devlin took her arm, squeezed gently. 'Let's grab a coffee while we can.'

Another squeeze, then coolness where Dev's hand had been. 'Hello?'

'Not so fast.' Cass spoke across the space. 'Two-year-old girl, runny nose, harsh coughing and temperature of thirty-eight. Possibly another case of RSV. I've put her in cubicle ten, green zone.'

'Good.' Chloe was off her chair and heading to the little girl, relieved she had someone else to concentrate on.

Unfortunately, Devlin was right behind her as she walked towards her new patient. 'This RSV seems to be escalating. Other hospitals around the country are starting to report a higher than normal rate for this time of year.'

Chloe's heart sank. 'The toddlers always seem to be the hardest hit with it. Though we did have a fifty-six-year-old woman on Friday night with symptoms. I didn't hear the outcome as I signed off shortly after she was admitted.'

'If that was the woman from Petone, then, yes, she's got the virus,' Cass told them as she held the curtain back to expose a tiny tot curled up on a woman's lap, tears streaking her scared face. 'This is Kiera and her mother, Megan. Devlin's your doctor for now, Megan, and this is Chloe, the nurse who's going to look after Kiera.'

Troubled eyes locked on Devlin, who found a smile as he studied the little girl Megan was holding gently. 'She's never been sick like this, Doctor. She never gets sick at all really. She woke me up with her coughing and crying. I might be panicking but I put her in the car straight away and drove here.'

'You did the right thing, Megan.' Devlin crouched down so he was looking directly at the child. 'Hello, Kiera. You don't feel good?'

Kiera turned her face into her mum's breast.

'Was she all right when she went to bed last night?' he asked Megan as he reached for the little arm closest to him. His finger found Kiera's pulse and he timed the beats.

'She was grizzling but I put that down to the fact she'd been at the play centre for longer than usual because I had to work extra hours as someone was away. She gets tired if she's there longer than six hours. Did I get that wrong?'

'It's not a case of being wrong,' Chloe told her, since Devlin was focusing on the pulse rate. 'You know your daughter better than anyone else. You know when something's not quite right.'

Devlin stood up. 'Chloe's got a point. Chances are Kiera didn't even have a fever last night. If her temperature was raised, it might've been only infinitesimally high. But it is high now. We are going to attach her to the monitor so we can keep reading her heart rate and BP. I want her temperature taken hourly, more if it rises any further, Chloe.'

Chloe brought the monitor across. 'Let's lie Kiera down on the bed. Megan, we need to get those thick clothes off her to help lower her temperature. While you're doing that I'll get some water. She needs to drink little and often to avoid dehydration.'

Kiera grabbed at her, crying out, 'Mummy.'

'Shh, sweetheart. Mummy's here. We're going to put you in the bed.'

'I want to go home,' coughed the wee girl.

'Nasal oxygen, please.' Devlin took the monitor leads Chloe held out to him and began placing them on Kiera's little chest as her mother removed her upper clothes.

'Be right back.' Chloe headed for the trolley with the oxygen tank and bags of nasal tubes. That poor child was scared and gasping for air, her face scorching red, as was the rest of her upper body now that they'd got her clothes off. Chloe grabbed a jug of water and a paper cup as well. 'Here we go. Megan, can you get Kiera to take a few sips of water while I set up the oxygen?'

'Water's not her favourite drink.' Megan managed a smile as she took the cup and jug from Chloe.

'Sorry, but it's better than a sweet drink at the moment. It's absorbed quicker and that's what she needs right now,' Devlin explained.

'Devlin, got a moment?' Cass asked from the corner. 'I want you to see another patient who's just been brought in.'

'Sure. You got this, Chloe?'

'Absolutely.' She wasn't leaving Kiera for a moment. Not until they'd got fluid into her and the oxygen flowing properly anyway.

'Good. I'll be back.'

* * *

'How's Kiera doing?' Devlin asked Chloe forty minutes later.

'She's settling down well,' Chloe answered. 'I've left her with another nurse for now.'

He held up a vial. 'Check this dose with me.' He breathed deep, savouring the light floral scent wafting from Chloe. Her abrupt change of mood before had him wondering if he'd been the cause for some reason, though she appeared to have calmed down now. Thank goodness, because he enjoyed working with her.

'Sure.' Her fingers brushed his as she accepted the vial he held out.

'Hey, I missed you over the weekend.'

Her eyes widened as they locked on him. Her tongue licked the corner of her delectable mouth.

'You were angry earlier.'

Her lips pressed together, moved left then right, opened. 'I'm confused, frustrated. I don't know what I'm doing, what you're doing, where we are.'

He got where she was coming from in spades. 'You and me both.'

'Oh, Dev.'

He pulled her into the supply closet, then kicked the door shut, enclosing them in darkness. Reaching for her, he found her mouth through sheer instinct and kissed her as though she was the only thing on earth that mattered. Which, at this point in time, she was.

CHAPTER SEVEN

'GENIE, THE LAST thing I need right now is a walk.' Chloe stared down at her pet sitting wagging her tail and holding the lead in her mouth. 'I'm tired and hungry. It's been a big day.' The patients hadn't stopped coming. No sooner had they sent one to Theatre or a ward and another two would arrive. She'd stayed on for an extra two hours helping catch up.

Wag, wag, wag.

'Yeah, I know. You don't care. I'm a broken record.' A tired smile finally made its way across her mouth and she reached down to rub Genie's head. 'All right. You win. As always. Let me get my walking shoes on. And a coat.'

More wags and a head nudge. Genie always knew when she'd got her way.

'We'll go into town and along Courtenay Place.' The beach wouldn't be fun in the rain, and sand would stick to Genie to make a mess back in the house. Never a great look. 'I can grab something to eat at the supermarket.' She was too damned tired to be bothered what she got, as long as it kept the hunger gremlins at bay.

Genie's ears had pricked up. Somehow she always knew words to do with food.

Pulling the laces tight on her second shoe, Chloe stood up and stretched her back. 'Let's do this before I change my mind.' Not that she would. Genie needed the walk, and it wouldn't hurt her. 'Wonder what Dev's doing?' He'd left the hospital before her, since the doctors had been up to speed with patients and his shift had long finished.

Her phone rang. 'Speak of the devil.' *Down, heart.* 'Hello?'

'Hey, like to share dinner somewhere?' Dev sounded breathless. Couldn't be because he'd been doing a workout in a gym. Not his style at all.

'I'd like that.' She'd love it. Did kisses come as an entrée or dessert? 'I'm just taking Genie for a walk, then I'll be free.'

'You're not going to the beach in this weather, are you?'

It was drizzling and chilly out there. 'I'm heading downtown to keep under the shop awnings. Want to meet me somewhere? There are some good eateries on Courtenay Place.'

'What about Genie? We can't leave her sitting outside while we have a leisurely meal.'

She'd forgotten her girl in all this. 'So want to pick me up after we get back from the walk?' Another idea popped into her head. 'Or we could get Thai and bring it back here.'

'I'd like that. I'll meet you in town, then walk back to your house with you.'

'Fine,' Chloe said. Then looked at her old jeans. Not up to speed if she was meeting up with Devlin. It couldn't hurt to impress him a little. Changing into the new pair she'd bought in a sale last week, she chose a soft cream blouse and navy woollen jacket.

Outside, Chloe pulled the collar of her jacket tight around her neck and stretched out her steps. The sooner they were under the cover of shop awnings, the better.

Genie didn't seem at all worried about getting wet, just trotted alongside her, sniffing the air every time they passed a takeaway outlet. And when they joined Devlin, she began bouncing along as though she'd caught up with her best friend.

Once they'd ordered their meal they continued walking.

'How do you cope with days like today?' Chloe asked. 'I'm talking about the toddlers with RSV.' Not that stolen kiss. 'It's heartbreaking seeing little kids so unwell.'

'By going for a long walk usually with music playing in my ear and breathing in normality.'

She hadn't noticed the earplugs hanging from his shirt pocket before. 'Joe Cocker by any chance?'

'You remember?' He grinned.

Heat scorched her cheeks. Was he referring to her dancing naked to Cocker's music in Devlin's apartment, and making love with him on the rug afterwards? 'Didn't I buy you a collection of his records when you got that ultra-modern stereo?' Records had started making a comeback and Dev had been into them big time. She'd been happy knowing there was something she could buy him he'd really enjoy and it had nothing to do with spending lots of money.

Dev was still grinning. So he did remember that afternoon. 'I've still got them all.'

So he was still into the records. That was good, as he hadn't had many interests outside medicine and family duties. Still into sex on the floor? She swallowed hard.

He continued, 'There's a shop in Queen Street that specialises in records. I bet they're making a killing. Good old vinyl is so popular these days. Not very practical when wanting to listen to music while going for walks though.'

Damn but she loved that grin. Always had. Probably the first thing she'd loved about him. And everything else had been right behind. They'd only taken days to get close and personal and start talking about moving in together. In hindsight, it had been way too soon. They should have taken their time getting to know each other better first. He might have trusted her more then. 'Half the population would think you were talking about something that covers the laundry-room floor.'

'True. Are you saying I'm old-fashioned?'

'More of a Neanderthal.' Though she had always enjoyed listening to music with Devlin, to her there wasn't a lot of difference between LPs and CDs. Except the expense. And dollars had been in short supply for her back then. Still were compared to what Devlin was used to. The difference in their incomes hadn't really bothered her when she'd loved him so much, and it had certainly not been the reason she'd agreed to get engaged to him. Something his mother had implied more than once. Mrs Walsh hadn't understood that growing up poor had never made Chloe envious of the wealthy, and certainly hadn't meant she'd ever get married just for the money. Devlin had believed her about that, something she'd always appreciated.

'No, Genie.' She twitched the lead to emphasise the order, and Genie stopped sniffing the shop doorway and moved on.

'What do you do in your spare time?'

'General household chores, and maintenance. There's always something needing to be repaired around the house. Waterproofing windows, replacing roof tiles and rotten boards, paintwork inside and out.'

'Sounds like you really enjoy doing all that.'

'I do. I've found immense satisfaction in turning my house into a home.'

'I can understand that. You've done something for yourself and it's turned out well. And you've always wanted a home of your own after your unsettled lifestyle as a child.' He looked pleased. For her? Or because he was hoping he might find something similar with his move to Wellington?

'We should turn around. Our takeaways will be ready soon.'

A warm hand took her cold one, wrapped gentle fingers around her rigid ones. As he used to take hold of her whenever she'd been upset about something. 'I know you struggled with your past and the people who never accepted you as part of your mother's life or for other reasons. I haven't forgotten any of the stories you told me about being rejected by the men who wanted Joy to live with them but not you. How could I when they made me angry for you? Hurt for you? I also recognised that they'd made you the woman I intended to marry and live with for ever.'

Thank goodness they were walking on a busy street as workers made their way from offices to bars and restaurants or bus stops. Otherwise she might've spun into Dev's arms and clung to him, hugged him until the chill that had been in her heart from the day they broke up finally dissolved. To hell with it. She threw her arms around him anyway.

'I'm glad you came to town.' What else could she say when her heart was in her throat? Devlin had loved her back then. The way he'd looked out for her, talked her through things that upset her, gave her confidence whenever it was lacking, had spoken loudly of his feelings, with open, loving affection. But he still hadn't been able to believe she hadn't been unfaithful to him. Was some of that her fault?

Had she done something to make him believe she didn't love him as much as he'd loved her? Had she been too accepting of everything he'd said, and not fought hard enough to make him see how wrong he was? Had she put on her 'I'm not good enough for you' hat and let him win the battle too quickly, too easily? 'I'm sorry.'

Devlin's hold tightened around her and he gazed down at her. 'For what, Chloe?'

Tell him. She looked up at him, locked her eyes with his.

He was waiting, quietly, expectantly.

Maybe this was just one more piece of the past she needed to let go of to be able to feel free of him.

You're never going to. He's inside you, in your head and heart.

'For not trying harder to make you believe me. I accepted too quickly that I didn't stand a chance of changing your mind so I gave up.' A gutless reaction that came from a time when getting away from people who didn't want her as a part of their lives was the norm. She should've trusted that Dev wasn't like that, but then Stephen had begged for a second chance and she'd trusted that he'd changed, and look how that had turned out.

'There were two of us in that story. Yes, you could've kept trying, but I still wouldn't have believed you. I accepted your guilt far too easily, and I'll have to live with that every day.'

'Oops, sorry, wasn't looking where I was going,' a young woman dressed in a business suit said as she bumped into them.

'It's fine. We should've found somewhere less busy for this conversation.' Devlin wrapped his arm around Chloe's shoulders and they began walking back towards the Thai restaurant.

Would her stomach be okay with receiving food on top of the emotions tripping through her at Dev's words? She'd try, just as she'd try to understand why he hadn't fought harder to save their future. At least she'd tried.

'You're overthinking everything,' he said close to her ear. 'But then you always did.'

Devlin frowned. He knew he'd walked away from Chloe too readily. He had been fore-warned and therefore prepared to see her with another man after his mother had warned him that she wasn't always the good girl he'd believed her to be. The thing was, he'd never thought of Chloe as good, nor had he wanted that in his girlfriend. Good spoke of dull and conventional, and not up to a bit of fun. It also didn't mean being unfaithful. He'd been so stupid; why had he taken his mother's word for fact and not dug deeper? That was something he would follow up on now. Mothers were supposed to support their children, not undermine all their dreams and hopes.

Devlin shuddered to think he might've made the biggest mistake of his life seven years ago.

Years wasted because he'd never stopped to consider that Chloe was innocent.

'Chloe, I should've stopped and listened to you, not walked away head held too high, thinking I was right and you were wrong.'

'Yes, you should,' she said gently.

They reached the Thai restaurant. 'You stay with Genie. I'll grab the food.' The dog was looking impatient to keep moving. Probably ready for her own dinner and to curl up somewhere warm.

'Sure.' Chloe drew a breath. 'Dev—'

There she went again. Dev. His toes tingled. He loved it. Warm fuzzies filled him as memories of wonderful times spent with Chloe rose. 'Yes?'

'Do you honestly, truly accept that I didn't play around on you?'

'Yes, I honestly, truly believe you didn't.' It was true. Completely and utterly true. He did accept it. He breathed easier than he had for days. His chest filled with oxygen and hope. His head swam with a longing he hadn't known in for ever. In seven years, really.

You're jumping in where you haven't been invited. Rushing towards Chloe and what you used to have without thinking it through.

He frowned. He didn't want logic to intrude on this moment, but it seemed his brain was insistent on applying caution this time even though his heart seemed to be stubbornly clinging to the hope.

'You want me to go in?' Chloe asked with a frown between her beautiful eyes.

'No. I've got it.' It might be taking him a few minutes to remember why they'd stopped outside a Thai restaurant but, hey, he was on to it now. His feet were bouncing as he entered the building.

They didn't stop bouncing on the way back to Chloe's small cottage, or when he followed her inside and closed the door behind them. It was like coming home, except Chloe hadn't owned a house when he first knew her. When they'd been together they'd spent many nights in his apartment in St Helier's, overlooking the Auckland Harbour. Posh, she'd called it. Normal, was his response. She'd frowned at that, but did her best to make herself comfortable, though sometimes he'd thought she preferred her cramped one-bed flat.

Chloe tapped his arm. 'I'll feed Genie, if you want to grab some plates from the cupboard. There's an open bottle of Chardonnay in the fridge if you'd like a glass. No red, I'm sorry.'

'Chardonnay's fine.' So might salt water be at the moment. 'Shall I pour you one, too?'

Her eye roll had improved with time. Sarcastic and cheeky all rolled into one. 'What do you think?'

'I'll take that to be no, then.' He looked around the neat kitchen space and figured the cupboard above the fridge might hold glasses.

Neat? Sort of. Devlin took another look. Everything was in its place. The glasses in the cupboard he opened were lined up, but not as perfectly as they once would've been. The wooden shelf gleamed but there was a hint of dust towards the back. Control freak Chloe had backed off somewhat when it came to keeping her life orderly. She'd driven him crazy with her need to have every single item in the kitchen, lounge, bathroom, bedroom, in the right place, facing the correct way. It had been her way of controlling life, of stating, 'I am Chloe Rasmussen. Don't mess with me.' Seemed she didn't need to put that out there quite as strongly any more. She'd found her strength inside herself. It had always been there, though too easily knocked aside when she was younger.

A wave of pure happiness for Chloe washed over Devlin. He was glad. She deserved to be able to stand on her own two feet and face, without flinching at, everything the world liked chucking at people. Though if he still knew anything about her, she'd be holding her breath at the same time.

'What's up? You forgotten how to pour a glass of wine?'

The bottle was in his hand, the glasses on the bench before him, and, yes, he was in la-la land. Again. 'Want to show me?' At least they could still tease each other and not wonder where it might lead. But, hell, he so wanted it to lead to her bedroom.

The bottle hit the rim of one of the glasses, shattered it into countless shards. He was mortified!

'You've definitely forgotten.' Chloe laughed. 'Give me that before you do any more damage.'

'Sorry. Where's the dustpan?' Chloe wasn't about to get glass in her fingers. What had happened? His brain had bombed out over the idea of getting closer to Chloe. Hadn't he decided to keep the lid on his emotions around her? Time to suck it up and get on with being friendly but not too friendly.

'Here.' She was holding a brush and pan out. 'Though looks to me you shouldn't be allowed near that mess. Might cut yourself.'

That'd wake him up in a hurry. 'I'm fine.'

'If you say so.' She reached for the second, still-in-one-piece glass and put it at a safe distance from where he was cleaning up. Then she got another out of the cupboard and filled them both with the wine. 'There. That's how it's done.' Her cheeky grin hit him hard.

'I learn something new every day. Got anything I can wrap the glass in?'

A roll of paper towels appeared. 'Go easy or I might have to do some stitching on your hands. Although, if I did, you'd actually be impressed at my skill.'

'That's right, you did mention you made your own clothes now, but I'm still trying to picture you at a table operating a sewing machine.'

'Peek in the second door on the right past my bathroom and you'll believe it. There's fabric for every occasion in there.'

'Any other skills you gained over in Italy you'd like to mention?'

She locked her eyes on him and laughed. 'The only one I'll admit to is that I learnt to live without all the hang ups I used to carry around.'

He wouldn't think about what else she might've got up to. Instead, he smiled and said, 'You wouldn't have laughed about that before.'

'No, I wouldn't have.' Her laughter didn't wane at all. Those eyes he'd never quite forgotten still sparkled with happiness and amusement.

'You're pleased to be able to surprise me, aren't you?'

'You bet.' Turning away, she got out plates

and cutlery, and began taking the food containers out and removing the lids. 'This smells so yummy. We'll sit at the counter.' She set two places side by side, though not so close they'd touch each other every time they moved.

Not across from one another at the table? Too intimate? But then Chloe wasn't acting as though she wanted to get close to him. Wise woman. There was nothing to be gained other than more heartbreak. Because despite how he was coming to feel for her, getting back together wouldn't be wise. Too much water had flowed under the bridge. He might have apologised for his mistakes, but would they be thrown in his face every time they had an argument? Even if she was interested in trying again, would she ever really trust him with her heart again after he'd let her down so badly? Did he deserve her to?

He handed her one of the glasses, and carefully tapped it with the second one. 'Here's to catching up, and to working together.' That was the right tone, wasn't it? She couldn't get upset about that, surely?

Chloe tapped back. 'To us.' Her lips touched the rim of the glass.

And his stomach did a backward flip. Those lips used to be manna from heaven on his hot skin. Man, could they work him up into a state in no time at all. Sinking onto a stool beside the counter, he dragged his hungry gaze away to focus on the rice and green curried pork. At least, that was what he thought he was looking at. Not that the food was making him feel any less wound up.

For all he knew, the takeout could be something Genie had dragged in. The longing for Chloe was blotting out everything else in his head. This was going to be the longest meal he'd ever eaten. And probably the most tasteless. 'Can I put some music on?'

'Help yourself to my sound system,' she replied over the rattle of dog biscuits filling Genie's metal bowl.

'You've got Joe Cocker.' His heart rate started increasing as he flicked through the options then turned up the volume. Cocker and Chloe dancing naked went together as did cheese and macaroni.

'Yeah.' She laughed, leaning one hip against the counter and raising her glass to those desirable lips.

He was incapable of stopping himself. Ignoring every single thing he'd just told himself about holding back from her, he crossed the room, taking the glass from her hand and leading her into the centre of the lounge. 'Remember this?' he whispered in her ear.

Her head nodded against his chest. 'Of course.' And then she was swinging her hips and kicking off her shoes, all in one graceful and sexy move.

His heart landed in his throat. His body tightened. And tightened some more as her arms rose above her head, lifting that figure enhancing blouse to expose skin. Warm, soft skin his fingers remembered too well. 'Chloe,' he croaked. 'Please stop, unless—' His throat blocked the rest of his sentence.

'Unless what, Dev?' Her voice was a purr as she danced in time to the croaky voice coming through the speakers.

'Damned if I know,' he growled and reached out to her.

She shimmied up to him, rubbed her belly against him, tightening him further. 'I don't know if this is right or wrong. I only know I want you right now, Dev. I need you.'

'Likewise, Chloe.' With that, he let go of the last knot in his heart holding him back and hauled her up against his whole length, lowering his mouth to claim hers. Tomorrow was another day.

Their bodies moved in unison to the rhythm beating through the room. Their mouths held each other, touching, tasting, feeling, remembering, creating new sensations. And when they couldn't take any more Devlin lifted Chloe in his arms and laid her on the rug in the centre of the room, leaning over her, reaching for the buttons preventing access to her hot pink skin.

Chloe brushed his hand aside, slid one button free, and ran her fingers over his face. The next button and she touched his chest with feather-light softness. The third button and her hand wrapped around the bulge pushing out the front of his trousers.

Taking a lace-covered nipple between his teeth, he nipped and licked. Held her arms above her head to give him time to bring her to a first climax while some of his control still remained. Her body shuddered and strained against him, her eyes wild with desire.

Somehow her hands were free and pulling at his belt, shoving his trousers down, reaching for him to hold and rub and squeeze, rushing him towards his own climax. Kissing a trail from her breast to her navel to the edge of her lacy knickers, he held onto the need threatening to explode out from where her hands were working their magic. Then somehow they were together in all senses of the word, their bodies joined, moving in a rhythm all of their own.

And then he knew; *this* was home.

* * *

Chloe closed her front door behind Devlin and leaned back against it, deafened by the pounding in her chest. Dev had just spent the last three hours here, in her house. They'd made love on the rug to the sound of their favourite music. They'd finally shared their takeaways at the counter, drinking wine and talking almost nonstop, and then gone to her bedroom and loved each other again with abandon.

The Devlin she remembered never lost track of what he was up to. Ahh, except when he was making love and losing control of his emotions. Oh, yeah, then he was a different man. One she could lose herself in all too easily. She had to stop going on memories and live with the updated version of the man who'd once meant everything to her.

She'd tried so hard to keep her distance from him, but now she'd given in, it wasn't enough.

A groan escaped her lips. She was done for. Back in love with the only man who'd ever made her feel special and loved and wanted. Back in love? Or had she never left? Thought she'd already worked this out. Didn't matter. She'd also decided not to do a thing about it because she needed to protect her heart, and here she was regretting letting Devlin leave the house after dinner.

The phone played its rock tune signalling a call.

'Go away. I'm not in the mood for talking.' But she headed to the kitchen where the phone lay on the bench. It might be Devlin. Hope dropped away. 'Hi, Mum. How's things? You're still taking it easy, I hope?'

'You think I'd get away with doing anything when Jack hovers around all the time, making sure I barely move off the couch from one hour to the next? I swear when I'm up and about properly he's going to regret being so caring, yet totally bossy.'

'You wouldn't change a thing.' Even to Chloe's ears, her laugh was a bit sharp.

'What's up?'

'Nothing.' Like her mother was going to believe that. 'I might be coming down with a cold.'

'That's why you sound tense and worried? Come on, spill, my girl.'

No getting away from this. 'Devlin was here. We shared a takeaway.'

'You're getting along all right, then?'

'Unbelievably well, which is hard to get my head around.' Kisses all round. Throw in making love. Yes, they were getting along just fine.

'You thought you'd both be sniping at each other because of the past. I understand that, but it has been a long time. I know how much you've grown and changed. Can the same be said for Devlin?' Her mother had always adored Devlin and had been devastated when his accusations had come to light. After that she hadn't had a good word to say about him. Actually, she hadn't said much at all. Protective mum to the fore.

'It's not so obvious, but yes, he seems less wound up and more at ease with who he is and what he's doing.' Pants on fire. If that reaction to her naked body wasn't obvious then she was on another planet. Deep breath. 'Like he's the Devlin I always thought was there, waiting to qualify and settle into the life he'd dreamed of.'

'It's possible these years apart have been good for you and your relationship.'

Chloe stared at her phone. Did her mother have some power that let her 'see' things? Putting the phone against her ear again, she asked, 'Did I hear right? You think Devlin and I could make a go of being together again? When you never had a nice thing to say about him after he kicked me out of his life?'

'What Devlin did was wrong. I told him so.'

'You what?' This was something new.

'I went and saw him, told him he had no right to insult my daughter like that, and he'd better sort his act out. Oh, and I added that he would never be welcome in our family again. I'm sorry, I shouldn't have done that, but he had to know who was right, and that you came first. Always.'

Her mother's loyalty had been unfailing throughout her life. As was Jack's. She couldn't help smiling.

'Thanks, Mum.' She'd expect nothing less. Even when it was her job to stick up for herself. Her mother was the best. 'But you just said our relationship might have gained something for the time that's gone by.'

'Yes.' Then her mother was silent.

Chloe waited.

'You met Devlin too soon. You were still finding your feet after Stephen, you were deep into your nursing training, and weren't really ready to settle down for good. Devlin was busy training to become a doctor, then an emergency specialist, and that took a lot out of him. Plus he had an extremely demanding family to deal with. Naturally you've both changed, matured, so it's possible those feelings you had for each other could always come back.'

Come back? They hadn't really gone away, as far as she was concerned. Not, not telling her mum that. 'Mum,' Chloe growled. 'You're thinking I want this to happen?'

'I have known you all your life.'

Therein lay the problem. Her mother rarely got things wrong about her daughter. Still, it didn't mean her mum was right about her and Devlin though.

Except she'd already admitted she still loved him. *And* kissed him like they belonged together, made love with him like there was no tomorrow. 'I've got to go. Genie needs to go out before settling in for the night.'

'It's barely gone eight o'clock.' Her mother laughed.

'I'm tired. We have the RSV filling the wards and our department.' Throw in nine people from a bus that rolled off the Remutaka Hill, two suspected cardiac arrests and a few other minor problems and there hadn't been time to think, let alone keep her energy levels at a peak.

'Just don't make any rash decisions.'

Too late. Maybe not a decision exactly, but her body had certainly shown her beyond doubt how she felt about Dev. 'No, Ma. Talk tomorrow.' If it was a little quieter than today, and *if* there were no distractions in uniform looking so sexy her blood didn't cool once all shift.

'I'll phone you.' Which meant there was no avoiding her mum and all the questions she'd probably come up with overnight.

Heading for the bathroom, Chloe flicked the shower on to hot and stripped off her clothes, rolling her aching shoulders and tight neck. It had been a hectic thirteen hours. Spending time with Dev out of the department had been good for her soul, helped her unwind.

Standing under the gushing water, she closed her eyes and tipped her head back, drowning herself in the welcome heat.

Dev believed her. He accepted she hadn't done the dirty on him.

Her eyes flew open. He really believed her. She still struggled to accept that after all this time. Yes, he'd changed in lots of ways. And he was prepared to stop and listen to her, had admitted he'd been wrong and apologised. But there was still one thing she hadn't mentioned to him yet. How would he react when she told him about the baby she'd lost? Would he be relieved because they hadn't been ready to be parents yet? Hurt that they'd lost a child? Upset that she still hadn't told him when she'd had plenty of opportunity to do so after his arrival here? They were supposed to be friends, if nothing else. So why hadn't she told him? Had she still not trusted him to say and do the right thing? No, it was because she'd been reeling from his reappearance in her life and she'd been trying to find solid ground before having such an emotional discussion. Hopefully, he'd understand why she'd kept it to herself.

She was supposed to be so much stronger these days, and if she didn't try to build on what they had now, she'd never know if they could make it work. One thing she was absolutely certain of: she loved him. So they needed to be able to move forward without anything holding them back. Which meant telling him about the baby.

'Chloe, you're in charge of zone green today,' Devlin informed her as she entered the department at sixty forty-five the next morning. 'And before you even begin to think you're getting off lightly, we already have three toddlers and two sixty-year-olds with RSV and two men awaiting surgery after a brawl at a pub in the early hours this morning.'

'Knew I shouldn't have got out of bed.' She laughed, then blushed and had to look away.

Dev's eyes widened and a look of need flitted across them.

She smiled. Life felt that good this morning. But there was no time to do anything about that. There was work to do, patients to help, and a handover to deal with. 'Guess I haven't got time to grab a mug of tea, then.'

'There's one on the bench with your name on it,' Devlin told her. 'I saw you coming along the footpath as I entered the hospital.'

'You're a champ. It was chilly out there this morning.' She picked up the tea and took a sip. 'Perfect.' A good guess or he'd remembered how she liked it? More likely he'd observed her making her own over the last few days.

'Why do you walk to work in the dark and cold?'

'It's not far, and parking costs aren't cheap around here. I always drive if it's raining or when I'm on nights though. Don't fancy meeting someone after they've been drinking at a pub. You've been here a while, I take it?'

He was meant to start at the same time she did. 'Yeah, couldn't sleep.' Devlin glanced at her, looked away. 'Figured I'd be more useful in here than at home trying to work out how to fix the leaking tap in my kitchen. Remind me to call the plumber at a sensible hour, will you?'

'How long's it been dripping?' There was a collection of grips and vices in her garage for that sort of problem.

'It was like it when I moved in, but I've never got around to doing anything about it. For some reason it annoyed me more than normal this morning.'

'Nothing to do with your sleepless night?' She cracked him a grin. This should be good. He'd sworn he was exhausted when he'd headed home last night. 'I'll call in after work and see what I can do for you.'

The pen in his fingers slid onto the counter. Those beautiful eyes were on stalks. 'You what?'

'I'm amazing at plumbing.'

'And changing electrical plates,' Jazz said from the other side of the hub.

'That's illegal,' Dev said.

'Only if someone finds out.' Jazz laughed. 'Our Chloe's a whizz with all sorts of minor repair jobs around the house if you're in a spot of trouble.'

'Jazz, shut it, will you?' Chloe tried not to join in her friend's laughter. 'I only do the straightforward chores. Let me know when you're going to be at home and I'll drop around with my gear.' It was time she saw his apartment anyway.

Jazz piped up. 'She doesn't come with a tool belt on her hips.'

Devlin just shrugged, continuing to look bemused.

'Right, shouldn't we be getting the show on the road?' Chloe sat before a computer and brought up the screen. By the looks of things, ED was already near to full capacity and rush hour was only beginning. It was a rare day someone didn't crash a car, fall off a bike, or trip out of a bus on the way to work.

If only that was all, Chloe thought as, many hours later, she wiped down the fevered body of three-year-old Jarvis suffering from RSV. The virus had gone rampant this winter. 'Hey, little man, let me put this under your arm, okay? That's a good boy.' She slid the thermometer in place, and held it there, keeping an eye on her watch.

'Is he worse?' Jarvis's father asked. 'He looks redder than he did half an hour ago.'

'His temperature might be peaking.' It was another degree higher than the last reading. She only hoped this was the peak, and there wasn't worse to come. Forty point five degrees was too high, almost dangerous. 'I'm going to talk to the doctor.'

'Paediatrics is overflowing,' Devlin told her when he heard Jarvis's temperature was still rising.

She already knew that. It was the reason the emergency department was chock full. So was the waiting room, where more people were waiting to be admitted and seen by a doctor. 'Are they taking more patients, or do we keep them here?' A paediatrician had been in the department most of the day, trying to keep up with the stream of sick children.

'Clare is trying to arrange for them to go upstairs, but we're waiting on orderlies to set up extra beds.' Devlin yawned. 'And I thought yesterday was busy. Looks like we'll be here later than ever.'

'There goes fixing your leaking tap today.' She tried for a smile, pushing the exhaustion aside for a brief moment.

'Always another day. I'm not there to get annoyed by it so it doesn't matter. Anyway, you don't have to do it. I'll get around to phoning a plumber some time.' He stepped around the curtain of the cubicle where Jarvis lay curled up against his dad, looking frightened. 'Hello, Jarvis. I like your shirt. That elephant looks really cool jumping over the rocks like that.'

The little boy glanced at his shirt and back at Devlin.

'Is he going to be all right?' the father asked.

Devlin spoke in a steady voice that gave out confidence even when no one knew how long it would be before they could get Jarvis's temperature down or if it might go even higher. 'We have to continue monitoring his temperature. I hope to have Jarvis moved to the paediatric ward within an hour, where the paediatric doctors and nurses can watch him continuously. He'll be more comfortable up there without other patients coming and going and creating noise and distress. The children's ward is full beyond capacity, but it is still a much more comfortable place for him to be right now.'

'You haven't really answered my question.'

Devlin sighed. 'You're right. As long as Jarvis's temperature doesn't keep rising he'll be okay. It could take a day or a few days to get it back to near normal and until then he will be kept in hospital.'

'Why so many cases? Is this something new? I've never heard of it before.'

'The virus has been around for years, but normally we don't get an outbreak like this. It's affecting the youngsters and elderly in particular. We believe the children are hardest hit because of Covid and being in lockdown so much last year. They weren't mixing with other kids and, therefore, weren't building a natural immunity to various bugs and viruses.'

The father nodded slowly. 'That makes sense, I guess. Another thing to blame on Covid.'

Chloe agreed. 'There's been a few things we've all blamed on that virus. And still do.' The world wasn't out of trouble yet. She held a bottle of water to Jarvis's lips. 'Here, Jarvis. Drink some more water for me.'

Jarvis shook his head and pulled back from the bottle.

His father took it from her. 'Hey, Jarv, do this

for Daddy, eh? You drink some and I'll drink some from my bottle. Okay?'

Big eyes focused on his father, and Jarvis slowly opened his mouth. He took a few sips and pulled away.

'That's the boy. My turn.' The father picked up another bottle from the bedside table and took some gulps. 'See? I took some big sips. I want you to try to do that too.'

Jarvis didn't move. Stared at his bottle in his dad's hand.

'Go on. Give it a go.' Chloe held her hand up, ready to high-five him.

The boy tipped his head to stare at her.

For a long moment she thought he was going to refuse. She winked.

And finally, Jarvis took the bottle in both hands and drank some water.

'Go, man.' Reaching out with her hand, she tapped his. 'You are a star.' Until next time she needed him to drink some more. To the father, she said quietly, 'Keep trying to get him to take a few sips every little while. He's burning up so the more fluids on board, the better.' There was no chance Jarvis would drink too much. He just wasn't interested. 'I'll pop back in a few minutes. I've got another patient to see now.'

Devlin followed her out of the cubicle. 'You have a knack of getting little kids to do as you ask.'

'And I didn't even have to bribe him.' She stepped into another cubicle and up to the heart monitor attached to Daphne Harroway, very aware of Devlin right behind her. Did he want to be a dad some day? He'd be awesome. A great role model, supportive, loving and loyal; all the things kids needed and wanted. She'd been aware of him all day, even when they weren't working alongside each other. Seemed that he'd got under her skin and wasn't going anywhere. There to stay. Which didn't bode well for getting much sleep in the nights ahead. 'No changes.' Leaning close to their patient, she said, 'Daphne, can you hear me?'

No response.

Taking the woman's hand in hers, Chloe tapped her fingers one by one. 'Daphne, can you feel this? Squeeze my hand if you can.'

'Nothing?' Devlin asked. 'I'd be surprised if there was.'

The woman had been brought in from a car accident in an unconscious state and Devlin had diagnosed swelling to the brain, caused most likely by severe whiplash during the impact. There were no other injuries so they'd put her on oxygen and she was about to be moved to the neurology department.

'Have we been able to contact any relatives yet?' Dev asked as he read the monitor's print-out.

'The police said they've got an address for a son, but no phone number so they've sent a constable out to Lower Hutt to make contact.' She couldn't imagine being in a situation like this and not having her mother or a close friend at her side. It would be frightening, though she was thinking as if she'd be aware, which Daphne clearly wasn't.

'I'd annoy the hell out of you by talking at you until you came round,' Dev said quietly from the other side of the bed.

'Did I speak out loud?'

'You have the most readable eyes I've ever come across.' He grinned. Then he quickly looked serious again. 'I hope they find some-one to be with her soon. A familiar voice can sometimes get through to even the most dam-aged brain.'

A nurse appeared in the cubicle. 'Devlin, you're needed in Resus. Forty-one-year-old male, severe stroke.'

'Coming. Join me when you can, Chloe.' He was gone.

Almost as though he hadn't been there, except he had. Her skin told her so with the tightening it did, and how the hairs lifted whenever he spoke. 'Sure,' she answered to his back. Straight and strong. That was Devlin.

Reading the monitor quietened the sensations. The oxygen pump's steady in-out movements lifting and dropping Daphne's chest kept Chloe focused and soon thinking only of her patient and not one hot, distracting doctor.

Until her shift ended, and she was able to take a break, grab a coffee and something to eat before starting on the next shift to help out until the department became less like a warzone and more of a calm, quiet place for sick people to see a doctor and be monitored, discharged or admitted to another department.

'I thought Wellington ED would be a little less hectic than the last one I worked in,' Devlin said as he joined her and the other staff who'd agreed to stay on for a few hours. 'I couldn't have been more wrong if I tried.' He had a plate of food in front of him that was going to take an hour to get through.

'Why would it be any different?' someone asked.

'Wishful thinking on my part, I suppose.' His smile was tired, and those engaging eyes were less twinkly than usual.

Chloe guessed he felt as shattered as she did

as she bit into a bagel filled with chicken and salad. Everyone probably did, she admitted. They'd been working extra hours for a couple of days now. It wasn't the hours, or even the work, that got to them. It was the stress when a patient didn't make it out of the department alive, or when someone was so severely injured their future looked grim, or when one of those little kids with RSV was coughing enough to make their lungs scream with pain and their eyes spill buckets of tears as they clung to their parents in fear. Yeah, those were the things that exhausted Chloe, and the people she worked alongside. There was no getting away from the mental anguish. No one wanted to see a patient's pain, or their loved ones' distress. It was so damned hard.

But they all put on their smiley faces and got on with what was required.

And she still loved being a nurse. All of the job, not only the nice and fuzzy moments when she got to see a patient go home happy and out of pain or danger. Growing up and often feeling lonely, she'd still always wanted to help others, maybe because deep inside she'd felt they might return the kindness in some way. These days she wasn't hanging out for other people's acceptance. She had finally figured out that not everyone would like her and that was fine.

Chloe pushed her empty plate aside and sipped her coffee. Her stomach rumbled, still hungry. Reaching over the table, she snagged an egg sandwich off Devlin's plate.

'Hey, leave that. I'm starving,' he growled before biting into the ham sandwich in his hand.

'Me, too. I'll buy you a chocolate muffin if you finish everything on your plate.'

'Yes, Mum.'

'Ha-ha. You think?'

'What? That you could be a mum?' Devlin asked. Then his head reared back as shock struck. 'Umm, delete that. I never said it.'

'Why not?' Chloe asked around the sudden lump blocking the back of her throat. 'It's not an unreasonable question.' Most people would ask something similar if the conversation was heading in that direction. No one else was looking at them strangely. But she knew, deep inside where her heart was thumping, that he was thinking of her, and their past. They'd talked about children. Of course they had. They were going to get married and having a family was part of it. But now? Devlin had asked about her becoming a mother and then got flustered. She didn't follow where he was going with this, except to wonder if maybe he still did have feelings for her. 'I certainly hope I will have children some time.' She regarded the man before her, knowing he really was the only one she could ever contemplate settling down and having babies with.

When to tell him about the baby she'd lost? When she was surer of where they were going with this new relationship, perhaps? Or should she just do it as soon as their frantic work schedules permitted? What if she hadn't miscarried? She'd have been a mum for more than six years by now. Devlin would've been a dad. She closed her eyes. After all these years, she could still tear up thinking about that. Devlin holding his baby, cuddling and hugging, murmuring sweet nothings when baby wasn't sleeping, holding a bottle of warm milk to his or her mouth and watching as baby sucked and swallowed.

'I can see you on your hands and knees playing games with a couple of toddlers.' Devlin's shock was ebbing, being replaced with amusement. 'You'll be good at being a mum.' Not amusement, then, but something more like wistfulness.

If only he knew. 'I had a good role model.' This was getting harder and harder to continue talking about casually. 'Do you still think you'd like to be a father one day?' she asked.

'Absolutely. Whenever we used to talk about kids, I'd get quite excited. That hasn't changed.'

His smile was lopsided. 'Imagine where we'd be if we'd stayed together. Ankle biters distracting us left, right and centre.'

'That many?' She had to tell him about the miscarriage as soon as possible. But not here.

'Maybe.' He picked up another sandwich and started scrolling through something on his phone.

Conversation finished. Thank goodness for that. It couldn't do anything other than stir up feelings best left alone when they had to get back to the department soon. Up at the display cabinet she chose two muffins, zapped her card, and returned to the table. 'Here you go. Get that into you, and keep your energy levels up for the next few hours.'

CHAPTER EIGHT

'GET A GOOD SLEEP,' Devlin told Chloe as she clambered out of his top-of-the-range car outside her house. 'At least we've got a straight forty-eight hours off work.'

She leaned against the door, wobbly with exhaustion. 'Think I'll be comatose for all of that.' Shadows darkened her face and her eyes had lost all their sparkle.

It had been a long week, working so many extra hours he'd lost count. 'What about Genie?' He could see her standing on her back legs at the fence, waiting for Chloe with a lead in her mouth.

'The girl next door has been taking her for walks after school every day.' Chloe looked around. 'Hey, girl. Not now, eh?' She turned back to him. 'Thanks for the ride. Catch up later.'

'That's a date.' Driving away, he watched Chloe in the rear-view mirror as she went through her gate to be greeted by an exuberant Genie. Chloe leaned over her, rubbing her head, and no doubt murmuring soft words of endearment. 'Lucky dog.'

Within minutes he was passing the Italian restaurant where they'd had a meal nearly two weeks ago. Was it really only two weeks since he'd first seen Chloe performing compressions on that woman on ED's reception floor? Two weeks ago he'd never have believed he could get so rattled by her again. But he was, and nowhere close to getting over the feelings of need and love that filled him all the time. Yes, love. As in feel it in every bone of his body. As in want to look out for her, care for her, make sure she wanted for nothing.

He hit the brake too hard and the car lurched sideways. Belatedly turning on the indicator, he pulled to the side of the road, waited for a gap in traffic and turned around to head back to the restaurant. It was after eight in the evening. He hadn't eaten since midday, and doubted Chloe had either. Tired as they were, food was important, too. As were a long hot shower and fresh clothes. Anyway, they could sleep together in her bed. Okay, possibly after some activity but what better way to drift off to sleep than in the warm haze after sex?

Striding into the restaurant, he went straight

up to Giuseppe. 'Hello. I know you don't usually do takeaways, but could you possibly do a couple of meals for Chloe and me? We've been working every hour there is and are exhausted. I want to take some food to her house and make sure she eats before falling fast asleep on her face.'

Giuseppe studied him. 'I wondered why she hadn't been in this week.'

'It's been the week from hell, and every time she was asked to put in extra hours she agreed straight away.'

'That's our Chloe. Puts everyone else first. Right, we'll put something together for you both. What were you thinking?'

'Whatever is Chloe's favourite, and— I don't know. What's the dish of the day?'

'Fettuccine Alfredo.'

'Perfect. One of those, please. Unless that's Chloe's favourite and I need to order something else?'

Giuseppe was still watching him closely. 'She's into meatballs and tomato and garlic sauce. You don't know her that well, then?'

Here we go.

The family to the fore. He understood this man and his brother were like family to Chloe. He was glad she had people there for her, but he was here now. No point in getting on the wrong side of Giuseppe though. Nothing to be gained, and possibly a lot to lose. 'When I first met Chloe she didn't know Italian from Chinese, and that was just the food. She certainly couldn't speak a word of your language and now it appears she's as near to fluent it makes no difference.' A softness slipped through him. Chloe had grown a lot in the years he hadn't been a part of her life. Grown in ways he, and he suspected she, would never have guessed.

'*Sì*. Almost fluent. She's a very tough *signorina*.' Giuseppe was still watching him. 'You care about her?'

'Very much.' Shouldn't he be telling Chloe this first? But he was being studied like a specimen in a Petri dish and wanted Giuseppe to understand he wasn't playing games with Chloe. He was for real. 'We were a couple a long time ago, then broke up. Now I'd like to think we're starting out again.'

'She never talks about her past.'

'That's Chloe. Keeps things to her chest. I hurt her back then.' Something he was still getting to grips with, but did accept. Locking his own formidable glare on the man opposite him, he said, 'But I'm hoping she'll give me a second chance. Any more than that I'll leave to her to tell you if she wants to.'

The silence between them was accentuated

by one of those odd moments when the restaurant patrons all went quiet at the same moment.

Then Giuseppe nodded. 'Fair enough. Now, about the meals. They'll be about thirty minutes. Do you want a glass of wine while you wait?'

Relief expanded Devlin's chest. 'Thanks, but I'm heading home to get cleaned up. I'll leave you my phone number in case I fall asleep in the shower.'

He didn't fall asleep in the shower, as warm and relaxing as it was. But he was late picking up the meals because his mother interrupted his plans by phoning to ask him to go home next weekend to attend a dinner being put on in recognition of his father's support for the local school's new sports facility.

'That's very short notice, Mum.'

'I know, darling, but it's not as though you're busy with anything outside your work in Wellington. You haven't been there long enough to become involved in organisations, and anyway, what would be the point? You'll be moving back here before you know it.'

'You need to get that idea out of your head, Mum. As far as I'm concerned this is a permanent move.' Like Patrick's was to Melbourne.

'Now, now. You know you're just flexing some muscle, proving a point, since you didn't get the position at Auckland General you wanted so badly. You'll be back.'

He'd turned down the job after he'd been headhunted because he didn't see eye to eye with the hospital's CEO over patient numbers. The woman thought beds should be available for urgent cases only, and not those patients who had nowhere else to go. 'Right, back to the dinner. I won't be coming up. I've got other things on, including work. You have to accept I will not drop everything every time there's an event on that you're going to. I'm sorry, but that's over for me now.' Quite frankly, he didn't care any more. He'd given so much of his life to supporting his parents when it should've been the other way round.

'Devlin, I don't like your attitude. We expect you to be here.'

'I know you do, but I cannot, will not, hop on a plane every time you call. I can't do it any more. I need to live my life, not yours and Dad's. It's not what you want to hear, I know, but I am not a drone.' His stomach crunched. He did feel bad, but he'd been raised to feel bad when he didn't bend over backwards to appease his parents. He'd had it up to his throat and higher, trying to please them. He'd begun to wonder if they'd ever seen his life through his eyes.

'This is Patrick's fault. He's fooled you into thinking his way is much better. It isn't, Devlin.'

Since moving south and working with Chloe he'd already started to understand how much he'd fallen for the lies and false compliments back home.

'Devlin, darling, you mustn't think like that. I'm only asking you for what's best for the family.'

Here we go. Heard it all before. Far too often. 'Sorry, Mum, but I won't be there next weekend. Or any other in the foreseeable future. Now, I've got to go. I'm meant to be somewhere.'

'You've got a woman already? Who is she?' Was that hope or annoyance in her tone?

He couldn't tell. What was more, he didn't care. Which didn't make him feel pleased with himself, but he wasn't changing course. Chloe was getting dinner tonight, and he was delivering it. Chloe. Hell. His mother would have fifty fits if she knew Chloe was back in his life. She'd always thought Chloe wasn't good enough for her son. 'Got to go. Talk again.' He hung up before the usual tirade began in full.

He was going to take a meal around to the most amazing woman he'd ever known, and he was going to relish any time he spent with her.

He'd stuffed up completely years ago and now he wanted to make up for that. Both for Chloe, and for himself. *If* she'd let him back into her life as more than a work colleague and a friend.

His phone rang again as he was heading out to the lift. 'Devlin Walsh.'

'You're not asleep, then.' Giuseppe chuckled. 'Dinner's getting cold.'

As if. That was the last thing Giuseppe and Lorenzo would allow to happen. Guess that meant he'd passed the test. He had no doubt the Italian wouldn't be laughing if he disapproved of him. 'I'll be there in five.'

When Chloe opened her front door to his knocking, his heart hit the bottom of his stomach. Wrapped in a thick, shapeless sky-blue robe, her long hair hanging in wet lengths down her back, and her pale face devoid of make-up, she was it for him. This was Chloe as close to her real self as she could get. Memories of making love in the shower, of cuddling up on the sofa in their robes, of laughing and talking and kissing without trying to be perfect, flooded him. Time to stop remembering and start making new memories. If Chloe wanted to continue what they'd started, that was.

'Dev? What's wrong?'

'N-nothing.' Everything. Here was the woman he was meant to spend his life with. And he'd gone and blown that out of the water seven years ago all because his past experience with Cath had tarred her with the same brush and let him believe she'd hurt him. What had he done to them both? Suddenly, he hated himself. Thrusting the bag containing their meals at her, he turned to go home. He couldn't do this. Sitting across from her at the table while she sat there looking so loveable and warm and real would turn his stomach into a tight ball that wouldn't accept food, make his head ping off the walls with frustration and anger at himself for being such a fool. He waved over his shoulder. 'Enjoy your dinner.'

'Devlin, wait.' It was a demand, not a 'what have I done wrong?' query. So unlike how Chloe would've once spoken to him.

But no, he couldn't wait, or face her, or explain himself. This sense of failure was too raw, and too likely to cause trouble. They wouldn't be able to continue working together if Chloe knew how he felt about her. He'd have to quit his job and try to find another in the same region or pack up and move on again. After a few weeks? Giving up too quickly? It was so unlike him, he stumbled. 'I've got to go.'

A strong hand on his arm. 'No, Devlin, you don't. Come inside and at least have a drink.' She paused. Then after a moment, 'Please.' She spoke like a child begging someone to listen to her. And too many times she'd been denied.

His heart gave in. Hell, *he* gave in completely. Turning, he wrapped an arm over her shoulders, tucked her lithe body up against him, and took a step towards her home. And another, another. As though walking towards the noose, only it didn't feel terrifying. More electrifying and intense. As if there were a wall before him that he was going to step through and keep on going, with Chloe at his side. He was probably being a naïve idiot, but when his heart thumped and squeezed as though it couldn't get enough air to be going on with, he had to revive it.

And that meant going inside with Chloe and sharing dinner—for starters. His fingers pressed deeper into her shoulder, held her tighter and closer. As if he'd finally come home after a long and lonely journey going nowhere.

Chloe used her hip to shut the door, not wanting to move out of Devlin's embrace. She felt as though she'd crossed a line with him, and the silly thing was she had no idea what had changed. Why she felt this way when she'd already admitted to herself she still loved him was a mystery. Perhaps she should just kiss him?

One glance at his face had her wondering if

she'd be making the right move if she did. Devlin looked worried and frightened and—and
loving. Loving of her? There was no one else
here. But… What if—?

*Grow up, Chloe. Be the strong woman you've
become, not the self-doubting girl you once
were.*

With a dry mouth and trembling hands, she
placed the bag containing dinner on the side-
board and turned to face Devlin.

Those intense cobalt eyes were watching her
every move.

'Chloe?' he whispered.

That got to her as nothing else could. It was
Devlin from the past, holding her heart in his
hands. Slipping her arms around his neck, she
stretched up on her toes and placed her mouth
over his. 'Devlin,' she whispered in return.
'Devlin, I've missed you so much I can't tell
you how I feel,' said so quietly he probably
didn't hear a word.

Hands spread across her lower back, strong,
firm and large. Familiar hands that knew her
well, hands that she knew very well. 'Chloe,
sweetheart, I've missed you, too.'

Her head spun. 'Really?'

'Yes, really.'

She'd said that louder than she'd thought.
Maybe not such a bad thing after all. It was

fine. Nothing was happening, except they were holding each other and admitting they'd missed one another, that was all. Her mouth opened, her lips moulded to his, and she pressed in for a kiss.

Instantly Dev was kissing her in return, deep and full and filled with longing, passion and memories. They were kissing as though their lives depended on it. It was a kiss that went on and on and was even better than any of the kisses they'd shared so far. She never wanted to stop, or to leave his arms again. Even better, it seemed he felt the same.

There was still a lot between them that needed sorting out before they took this too far, but she was hopeful they'd get there.

Dev shifted, now holding her even closer to that warm, masculine body as he kept kissing her.

To hell with being sensible. It was impossible when she needed him, wanted his naked body up against hers. Now. He was the only one she'd ever known such longing and escape with. Twisting in Devlin's arms, she found a hand and began pulling him along to her bedroom. Bedroom? Who needed a bed for this? Stopping, she pressed him against the wall and returned to kissing him. Her hands tugged at his jacket, pushing and pulling it off his shoulders and downward until his arms were free.

Shucking it away, he reached for her, lifting her up against him, his mouth still covering hers, his tongue rediscovering hers.

Chloe cried against his lips. More, more, more. His skin was hot against her palms when she managed to shove her way under his clothing. His hard, throbbing need for her was pressing into her belly. Desire pulsed at her centre, ready for Devlin to join them together. Her fingers were thick and clumsy as she tried to undo the zip on his jeans.

His mouth jerked away from hers. 'Let me.' His hand pushed hers aside, then his jeans were sliding over his hips to his thighs, and beyond. And he was back to kissing her.

Even though it had only been a few days since they'd made love it wasn't enough. She'd missed this. Missed Dev. Missed *them*. Reaching for him, she wound her fingers around his need for her, absorbed the pulsing heat, the length, the passion she knew was coming.

Somehow without letting go of him, she managed to shove her knickers down till they reached her feet and she could step out of them, all the while sliding her hand up and down Devlin's response to her.

Then he was lifting her so she could wind her

legs around his waist and take him inside. Fast. Hot. Deep. Her body was imploding, her head wasn't thinking, and her heart was dancing.

'Chloe, love, wow.' Moments later, Devlin was still holding her tight against him, breathing fast, and looking astonished and happy.

Thankfully, happy. She'd fall apart if he hadn't been happy. 'Yeah, Dev, wow.' Placing a kiss on his chin, she smiled with everything she had. 'We're still so good together.'

'We sure are. I can't believe how we do that. Read each other so easily and quickly. It's how we've always been together.' Was that longing of another kind in his voice? In his eyes?

'It is.' Snuggling into him, she couldn't stop smiling. Everything about her was warm, soft, tender, and so happy. Yep, she too was happy.

Somewhere her phone was ringing. 'I'll ignore that.'

'Might be important.' Devlin leaned back to look at her in his arms. 'Seriously.'

Nothing could be as important as being right here with Devlin. Nothing. No one.

'Come on. You'd better answer it.' He was heading towards her kitchen, where she thought the sound was coming from, his arms still wound around her.

Glancing at the screen, she grinned. 'Giuseppe. Is that where you bought dinner?'

'Yes. Bet he's ringing to check up on me.'

'Why?'

'I told him to prepare your favourite meal plus something for me. I think he worries about you, though I was only bringing around dinner.' Heat suffused his cheeks. 'Which is probably getting cold as we stand here practically naked, staring at a phone you don't seem to want to answer.'

Laughing, she picked up the phone. 'Hey, Giuseppe, dinner's delicious. Nothing less than I'd expect. The company's good, too. Let's catch up when I'm not working crazy hours.' She pressed off and put the phone back on the counter. 'Okay?'

Shaking his head at her, he grinned. 'I'd better grab the food so we can eat. Can't have you lying to your friend.'

'I'll get you an old robe Jack keeps here for whenever he and Mum stay. As much as I'd prefer you remained naked, it isn't that warm in here.' She glanced across at the firebox and groaned. A few bits of well-burnt wood glowed but it wasn't exactly a roaring fire. 'I did light it when I first got home but there hasn't been much time to add more wood.'

'Genie's curled into such a tight ball I'm surprised she's breathing.'

'I'm more surprised she hasn't been nudging

me to do something about warming the house up.' That would've been an interesting interruption to what had been going on in the hallway. After handing the robe to Devlin, she threw a couple of pieces of pine at the firebox, rubbed Genie's head, and went to pour two glasses of Cabernet Merlot before sitting down to eat.

'You bought in red wine in case I visited?'

'Caught.' She grinned. So much for her plans of eating toast in bed before falling asleep for the next few hours. What an entrance Devlin had made. Food. Kisses to die for. And sex that cut through all the pain and cruel words of the past like a knife through soft butter. 'What made you decide to go buy me dinner instead of going home?'

'I was hungry, and I kept seeing your face, full of exhaustion, and figured, hey, why not share a meal together? It was something I could do for you.' Devlin drew a slow breath. 'Besides, I didn't want to go home to an empty apartment. Or stay there after I'd had a much-needed hot shower.'

He was lonely? Or at that point of tiredness where everything was too much of an effort to do just for himself? Winding her fingers around his hand on the counter, she said, 'I know that feeling. I'm glad you came back.' More than anything that's what had tickled her buttons tonight. Everything felt different between them. The underlying tension that crept up on her at unexpected moments at work seemed to have disappeared completely. Everything about her was relaxed. She was probably heading towards disaster. 'I mean that. We've got on well these past couple of weeks, but there have been times I've wondered where we might be headed. Now it seems like old times where everything happened fast and was so good.'

Careful, Chloe.

There was a lot to move on from still. Or was it best to let go of everything that had happened seven years ago, including the miscarriage, and just move forward? He had apologised for his mistakes. Going over and over what had happened and upsetting them both wouldn't be of any benefit to either of them and might even drag them down into a dark hole again.

Looking thoughtful, Devlin put the containers of food on the bench. 'Want these heated up? I'm okay with them as they are. We didn't spend a lot of time being distracted.' If he hadn't been smiling that gentle, loving smile she'd missed so much she might've wondered if he thought they'd been too rushed.

There was something he was avoiding saying. She still knew him that well at least. She also remembered that pushing him wouldn't get her anywhere, so, placing a hand on the container labelled meatballs, she shook her head. 'That's still very warm. It'll do fine.' She found plates and cutlery, and spoons to dish up. 'Let's eat. I'm starving.'

The silence between them as they ate their delicious pasta meals and drank their Cabernet Merlot was comfortable. An ease she hadn't felt in years. One she'd only known with this man, and then not often. Back then they'd both been busy with their careers, studying and working lots of shifts. There'd also been lots of questions for her about her future, mostly from his mother. Did she want to be a nurse once she was married, or was she going to become a society wife going to an array of functions to raise funds for those less well off? Her choice without a doubt was to continue in her chosen career. Nursing was so important to her, made her feel needed and filled her with joy at being able to help people who were medically in dire straits. It was hands-on caring, not anonymous support to people she'd never meet.

'You were never cut out to be like the women my mother mixes with.' Devlin was watching her as he forked up a mouthful of pasta.

'How is it you've always been able to read my mind so easily?' It was unreal at times. And a little nerve-racking. No secrets. Except, of course, the one time he'd misread her with dire consequences. But here she was, ready to try again. Try? Leap in, boots and all, more like.

'It's something we've always had. It was just there, if you remember.'

There wasn't much she had forgotten. Including how they liked to cuddle up in bed after making love, their legs entwined, arms around each other, and talk nonsense. 'Eat up. I'm shattered, and the bed's waiting.'

Devlin couldn't help thinking back to the many other occasions where they'd shared sex and a meal, and more sex, not least the night they'd spent together only a few days ago. And he couldn't wait to do it all again tonight. He forked up more pasta and sauce. 'Those guys really know how to cook. This is excellent.' So was Chloe. He grinned. Who'd have thought when he knocked on her door that they'd get wild and passionate within minutes? Certainly not him. He might've wanted it, but he would never have gone out to make it happen. But then, often when he and Chloe got together things just happened. They were meant for each other.

But he couldn't prevent a knot of fear from starting to wind up in his gut. Walking away from Chloe last time had decimated him. Even though he'd been proud and determined not to be taken for a ride by her, the pain of losing the love of his life, the woman he'd believed he'd spend the rest of his days with, had left him empty and bewildered. He couldn't face any of that again if this didn't work out for a second time.

Nor could Chloe.

'You've gone serious on me.'

'Sorry. I didn't mean to.' Which was true. Enjoying this evening was what was important. He did want to try again with Chloe. He'd stop overthinking everything and try to take it slowly.

A soft hand touched his. 'We're just being us. This is how we do things.'

He couldn't help himself. He laughed. 'You're right. So, let's finish up here and head to bed.' He wanted to make love to Chloe again, and sooner rather than later. And, honestly, he could do with some sleep. He'd forgotten how tired they'd been when they knocked off work. Too many distractions going on. Distractions he loved.

'The Devlin I know.' She was grinning and yawning at the same time.

Reminding him again that they both needed sleep. But it wasn't going to get in the way of him showing her how much he cared about her. He could do showing, but not telling. Not yet. That might take a little longer.

CHAPTER NINE

CHLOE STRETCHED HER legs to the end of the bed. At least she tried, but a big lump was in the way. 'Genie, what are you doing on my bed?'

'She's been there for a couple of hours,' grunted the other, warmer bundle beside her. 'I thought it must be normal for her to sneak onto the bed once you were asleep.'

'Yes, but I usually wake enough to send her back to her doggie bed. She probably thought if you're allowed here then why can't she join us?'

'And how do you explain that to a dog?' Devlin laughed.

'Down, Genie.'

'Like she's taking the slightest bit of notice, Mum.'

Chloe smiled and snuggled closer to that divine body. It was awesome having him here after staying with her the whole night, laughing, warm and cuddly in bed. This was something she hadn't had in years. Since he'd kicked her out of his life. The few men she'd dated and ended up in bed with hadn't given her the same sense of ease, of being at home and comfortable, and she'd never stayed with them all night long. Not one of them had attracted her in the off-the-chart way Dev did. He always had, and it seemed he always would. 'Genie, down.'

At the stronger command Genie slowly rose up and jumped down to the floor to stroll out of the room as though she were really the one in charge, not Chloe.

'Typical.' Rolling away from Dev before she lost her mind all over again, she tossed the covers aside and sat up. 'Better let her outside before there's trouble.' The last thing she wanted was any lovemaking to be interrupted by a dog with crossed legs. 'Want a cuppa?'

'Since it's the best offer I've had since I woke up an hour ago, I'll say yes.' Devlin shuffled up the bed and clasped his hands behind his head on the pillow.

Cheeky thing. 'Lots of milk and three sugars, right?'

He just laughed.

But he spluttered into his mug when he got exactly that. 'You— You—'

'Yes?' she asked smugly as she settled back into bed with her perfect cup of tea. 'Problem?' The laughter dried the moment he stood up from the bed stark naked. Her dream man. Not overly muscular but built exactly how he should be. From those gorgeous wide shoulders, his lean body tapered down to his tight abdomen, and beyond, to his strong thighs. Her mouth dried.

'It certainly appears you've got one.' He laughed. 'Would it be childish to say ha-ha before I go get a drinkable cup of tea?'

She finally managed to find her voice. 'Wouldn't matter if I said it was.' This was fun. Silly conversation, if it was even that, about nothing. Relaxing, endearing. Although she'd prefer it if that sexy body weren't striding out of her bedroom… 'Devlin,' she called seductively.

He flapped a hand over his shoulder. 'Keep your tricks to yourself. I'm getting a cuppa before I do anything else. Then I'm going to see what's in your fridge and pantry that I can cook for breakfast.'

Reality check. 'You'll need to go to the supermarket if you want more than chocolate cereal.'

He poked his head back around the door. 'You still eat that disgusting stuff?'

'I need a chocolate fix some mornings, all right?'

'Chloe, Chloe. How do you look so stunning and lithe while eating sugar-laden cereals?'

'By running around the emergency department non-stop for at least eight hours on end, five days or nights a week.' Snuggling down the bed, she drank her tea. Thank goodness for days off. She wasn't due back at work until tomorrow night and she'd make the most of her time. She and the girlfriends were getting together for a birthday lunch today, and she might see if Devlin wanted to go to dinner somewhere tonight. There was something else she had to do, if she could remember it. Apart from the usual walks with Genie and doing the loads of washing that had accumulated over the week, that was.

Devlin went past the door, a steaming mug in one hand. 'Genie's out in the yard. I'm grabbing a shower, then heading out to get some supplies.'

'Don't forget I'm going to fix your leaking tap too.'

He appeared in the doorway, all of his splendid body on display for her to ogle. 'I'll cook you the best breakfast you've had in a long time and you can deal with the tap.' He disappeared, taking her favourite morning image with him.

'Come back and make love,' she whispered to thin air as the bathroom door snapped shut. Guess that meant she'd better get up and start her day.

* * *

Devlin sat back and rubbed his stomach. 'Nothing like a full breakfast to start the day.'

'Not bad.' Chloe grinned around the forkful of bacon, egg and hash brown she was slipping into her mouth.

Cooking didn't used to be her thing, and from what he'd seen of her pantry and fridge still wasn't. There was a stack of heat-and-eat meals in the fridge, but no fresh meat and eggs. Not a lot of butter or cooking oil anywhere to be seen either, which said it all. 'So you didn't learn to cook while you were in Italy?'

A smug look filled her gorgeous face. 'I can do a mean pizza, a not too bad macaroni cheese, and even a pasta dish with packet pasta and tinned sauce.'

'But you can change tap washers. Guess we all have our specialities.' He enjoyed cooking. It relaxed him at the end of a hectic day, and gave him pleasure to eat something he'd put together.

Now he did the same for Chloe. At least, he hoped she'd be happy with his input to their morning. Speaking of which. 'You got anything planned for the day?'

'First thing is a walk with Genie. Might go past the supermarket to pick up a few bits and pieces. I'm out of soap powder, for one.'

'Nothing that needs cooking?' He ducked as a scrunched-up paper serviette came his way.

'There's heaps of food in the fridge.' Chloe shoved out of her chair and dumped her plate in the sink. 'You want some bones, Genie?'

The dog's wagging tail whacked the chair her owner had just vacated.

'Thought so.' Chloe filled her mug with more tea. 'More for you, Dev?'

'Nah.' He began rinsing plates to put in the dishwasher. 'Two's more than enough. I feel wired already.'

'So you won't join us for coffee at Bengie's? It's part of the walk routine on my days off.'

'Bring it on. Coffee is my preferred kick-start to the day.'

A small frown appeared on that beautiful brow. 'That's new.'

He had always been a tea man, but not any more. Coffee and more coffee, to the point he sometimes got a throbbing headache, but it was worth it. 'Shows I'm open to change.' Wasn't he? He thought so. He could admit to himself his feelings for this woman. That was a change in capital letters right there.

Biscuits clinked into the tin dog bowl. 'You moved from Auckland to Wellington, drink coffee when you barely used to touch it. What's next?' Her grin was mischievous. 'Let your hair grow below your shoulders?'

I'll tell you what could be next, if I can let go my fear of being hurt if this doesn't work out again.

Because even though he knew now that she hadn't done what he'd believed, he did understand how vulnerable he'd felt when they'd broken up. 'I was thinking more along the lines of getting a pet guinea pig.'

Her eyes were sparkling in the way that tightened his gut, and other places. 'Genie would have it in one hit.'

Genie stopped scooping up biscuits and looked at Chloe.

Chloe rubbed her head. 'Sorry, girl. Devlin won't be providing you with a live toy. Unless he gets a cat. Then there'd be some activity going on whenever we visited.'

She was intending to keep this relationship going? On what level? Friends or lovers? Which did he prefer? That didn't even warrant asking. He knew the answer. After last night there was no way he could walk away from her again. He either went into this full on or not at all. If he held a part of himself back trying to protect himself, too much hurt would ensue, and neither of them deserved that. 'Chloe.' He paused, his breakfast suddenly heavy in his belly.

Her head shot up, that twinkle in her eyes instantly replaced with caution. Doubt, too. 'Yes?'

Why had he started this? What was wrong with just getting on with the day? They didn't need to go over things again, or talk endlessly about the past. They could have fun, enjoy being together and see where it led, couldn't they? Except… 'We've done it again, haven't we? Gone fast and furious. No looking back or even sideways, just caught up in the moment, and now we've slept together again. That's twice within a week.'

Her knuckles were white at her sides. 'You're regretting making love?'

'No.' It was almost a shout. 'No, not at all,' he said a little quieter.

Her fists didn't relax one bit.

'I was thinking aloud. The first time we met and got together, it all happened so fast, like we were meant to be together.'

Stop. Take that back or you can't follow up. You'll put your big flat feet right in it.

Devlin looked away, came back to face Chloe. He didn't do avoidance any more. 'We seem to be doing the same thing again. But I don't want us to rush it too much this time. We need to get to know each other again.'

'I can understand that. I feel the same way,'

she said in a stronger voice than he'd expected, and with a direct look that said, *Don't mess with me*.

She was less willing to rush in and try to please him. Some of the tension slipped away. They still hadn't touched on their feelings for the situation or each other, but she wasn't going to let him walk all over her. He gave a mental fist pump. He'd loved Chloe before, and he liked this Chloe even more. He loved her. But that wasn't for saying. Not today. Not until he felt safe.

'When I learned you worked here, too, I admit to feeling knocked sideways. Suddenly I started wondering if there was something unfinished between us, when it had never occurred to me before.' He leaned his hip against the counter and folded his arms over his chest. And watched Chloe as he let go his hold on the words that had been building up for two weeks. 'I never believed we'd be able to have an ordinary, friendly conversation without accusations creeping in. Our break up was loud, nasty and complete, yet once I saw you the day you returned to work, I knew we weren't finished.'

Her hands tightened just as they'd been relaxing. 'We were over.'

'True. So why are we getting along so well? Hell, we made love twice on Monday night and twice again last night. We're planning on going out for a walk and coffee soon. You're going to fix my tap. What is going on?'

Chloe stared at him as though he'd grown a second head.

He waited. He'd put too much of himself on the line to go on without some hint from her that she might be feeling the same as him. She didn't know he was having doubts about himself. Any minute now she'd burst out laughing and point at the front door.

Two steps brought her to him, where she placed a hand on his chest.

She was being friendly, not sending him packing. That had to be good.

'It seems we just can't stay away from each other. Forget the last seven years.' Her shoulders dropped briefly. 'No, we can't forget what brought us to this point, and we shouldn't. We've both learned lessons from it. What I mean is we seem to have a knack of leaping into each other's arms without overthinking it. There is something between us that we can't seem to control. Like we're either meant to be together or we should live poles apart.'

'Exactly.' He could see in his mind's eye the first time he'd ever seen her. Chloe had been standing in her uniform on the opposite side of the ward where he was with a specialist learning everything he could. She was gorgeous and she'd had him hot in an instant, and he hadn't even known her name. He'd gone across and asked her out, and within days they were sharing a bed, and sometimes his apartment, and were never going to be apart again.

'Dev, I don't know where we're headed any more than you do. I do know I want to find out, though.' Her faced had paled, but determination highlighted those eyes.

He pulled her into him. 'Starting with a Genie walk, coffee and a dripping tap.' Man, he loved holding that soft, hot body, breathing in the essence that was this woman, knowing she was his other half—if only he could let go of the fear. His arms dropped away. But his mouth gave him away. He couldn't stay away from Chloe. 'Let's go out to dinner tonight. Somewhere down on the wharf, overlooking the harbour.' His heart was pounding. Would she or wouldn't she?

'I'd love that.'

Phew. The breath he'd been holding spilled out. 'So would I.' It was as close to mentioning love that he was likely to get for some time. But it was a start.

'I think we do need to slow down a bit, get to know each other more thoroughly. Not take everything at face value.'

'You think that's what we did last time?' he asked.

Chloe nodded. 'We got into a close relationship fast. We fell apart almost as quickly. Not once did we stop and consider what we were doing and what it all meant for each of us.'

His head dipped in acknowledgement. 'You are so right. Does slowing down mean I can't take you to bed and make you cry out with pleasure?'

'Do it slowly and I'll be very happy.' She grinned.

Chloe headed for the shower, a smile lingering on her mouth. Devlin was her man. How could she have thought otherwise? Or thought she'd stopped loving him? She'd been fooling herself for seven long, lonely years. He was her other half, her soul mate, her love.

He meant everything to her.

The hot water streamed over her achy body. Filling the palm of her hand with liquid soap, she massaged her arms, legs, stomach. Everywhere. All the while Devlin filled her head.

Dev, you make my heart sing.

And her head spin, and her stomach soft and gooey.

Her hand paused over her belly. Where a baby might one day grow. A baby. Perhaps it was something to look forward to in the future when they both were more settled in their new relationship. Her hand tightened briefly.

Her heart dived. She had to tell Devlin about the baby she lost. Had to tell him before they went any further. Despite her wondering if perhaps it might be better to draw a line under the past in case it overshadowed the present, there could be no secrets between them going forward. Time had healed most of her hurt, although it would never go away completely. She'd miscarried, accepted it after a lot of pain and crying, and had eventually moved on knowing that one day she'd still have a child if she met the man she wanted to live with for ever.

But the thought of telling Devlin was making her nervous, and she didn't fully understand why. He wouldn't be upset that she'd kept it from him; he'd understand that it was a sensitive subject for her and she'd needed to pick the right time to talk about it. She could have sworn there'd been a look of love in his face when they'd been talking. These past hours had shown that they could and did get on so well, that they knew each other beneath the exterior face they showed everyone else. So what did she have to worry about? Devlin would hug her, kiss her and accept that she'd coped.

Overthinking things again, Chloe.

She snapped the water off, grabbed a towel and rubbed herself dry hard and fast. In her bedroom she pulled on jeans and a thick red jersey, tied her hair into a ponytail, ignored the make-up on the shelf, and headed out to the kitchen where Devlin was wiping down the bench.

He looked relaxed and happy.

Chloe hesitated. This could wait. They were heading out for a walk and coffee. Why bring it up now?

Because I'm Chloe Rasmussen, the woman who doesn't dodge problems.

Anyway, there wasn't going to be a problem. They just had to discuss it and then draw a line under it so they could carry on getting to know each other again.

'What's up?' He was leaning against the bench, watching her.

'There's something you need to know before we go any further.'

'Sounds serious.' Caution was darkening his eyes.

'It—' Swallow. This shouldn't be so hard. 'It's important to both of us.'

'Go on.'

She had his undivided attention, and it didn't sit well. Again she wasn't sure why. Not when her biggest issue about their break up was how he'd refused to listen to her.

'Four weeks after we broke up I had a miscarriage.' There, it was done. Now he could hug her and say he was sorry to hear that, and how had she managed?

'You what?' He stood straight, his shoulders tight, his face blank with shock. 'I didn't know you were pregnant. Why didn't you tell me?'

'I didn't know myself.'

Hug me, Dev.

'You didn't know? How far along were you?' Now he reached over to caress her cheek with the back of his hand.

Some of her tension leeched away. 'The doctor thought seven weeks.'

'And you really didn't know?' Bewilderment blinked at her.

Similar to how she'd felt when the bleeding began. 'Not a clue. But life was a bit hectic around then. It never registered with me that I'd missed my period.'

'I suppose so.' He didn't believe her?

'Probably.'

Don't let him do this to you. Don't do it to yourself.

'It was a shock when the pain struck and I

started bleeding. I had no idea what was happening at first. I mean, as a nurse I did, but it was happening to me and I didn't even know we were having a baby.'

'Why didn't you tell me?'

Don't lose it. Stay calm. 'Dev, I tried, you know I did. More than once. I phoned, left messages, came around to your apartment and left a note. I even tried visiting you at work once. You refused to talk to me. I know you thought I was looking for a reconciliation, another chance—'

'Oh, my God,' he groaned, reeling back from her.

'But there was so much more to it.' Breathe slowly. In, out. In, out. 'I wanted you to believe me when I said I hadn't cheated on you.' In, out. *'And* I wanted to tell you about the miscarriage. Until then having a baby was something for the future, but the moment I understood what I was losing I was gutted. It hurt so bad, so deep, I became very withdrawn for a while. I wanted that baby. *Our* baby. I loved you, Dev. I still do.'

He continued watching her, his eyes tortured in a white face, holding himself tight, his hands now at his sides, flat and tense.

Reaching for his hands, she found them cold and shaky as though he was in shock. 'I do love you, Dev,' she repeated softly, and waited for his response. And waited.

She'd heard it said, but never believed it until now. Silence could be deafening.

Say something. Anything. Tell me you're falling in love with me again. Or that you don't think you can and you're sorry but you're leaving. Stop this silence. It's frightening me.

Finally he whispered, 'I am so sorry, Chloe. I should have been there for you, but I let you down so, so badly. It won't happen again.'

This crushed response was not what she'd hoped for. 'Devlin, I got through it. I'm here, happy, and stronger. You're here, and we're making inroads into fixing past mistakes. That's all that matters. I didn't tell you so you could take the blame or hate yourself. I told you because I don't want any secrets between us. It has always been something I wanted you to know if we caught up again. I just had to work up to telling you.' She paused.

She was talking to air. Devlin had gone, head bowed as though the weight of the world were on his shoulders, closing the door ever so quietly behind him. So quiet it spoke of finality. Dinner was clearly off.

She straightened her shoulders. 'I'm not giving up on you that easily, Devlin. You walked away from us once before. Don't think you're getting away with it a second time.' That would make both of them stupid and they weren't. Not even close. They belonged together through all the love and pain that life would inevitably bring them.

Chloe had been pregnant—with his baby.

Devlin strode down to his car, his neck tight with anguish as he fought the need to look back. He couldn't for fear he'd run up to her front door and beg to be allowed back in—into her life for ever. And he didn't deserve her.

He'd wrongly accused her of having an affair. Refused to listen to her telling him she had not, that she loved him and would never deliberately hurt him. He'd refused to hear she'd lost their baby which meant he hadn't been there to support her through what must've been agonising, both physically and mentally. She'd have wanted that baby. Absolutely. So would he.

He could feel her hurt now, understood it for what it had been back then, not what he'd interpreted it as. He'd thought she was just angry at losing him and her ticket to a better lifestyle. That had been his excuse to protect his already battered heart by not engaging with her at all. He'd thought she was the second woman to treat him wrong; he hadn't stopped once to think that he might've been hurting Chloe as much.

If only he'd known how much more he'd hurt her.

If he had listened to her just once, he might've been there to hold her, soothe away the agony of losing their baby, to reassure her they'd try again when they were ready. Instead she'd faced it all on her own. With her mother and Jack, most likely. But that wasn't the same as if he'd been there for her. He'd been her fiancé, he'd loved her. It had been his place and he'd relinquished it without realising. Which was not an excuse, because if he'd only paused to hear her out then none of this might have happened.

He slammed the car door and pushed the ignition button hard. He could hardly breathe. He had to get away. Put some distance between them while he absorbed what Chloe had told him and how terribly he'd let her down.

Something penetrated his agony.

She'd said she still loved him.

How could she? Couldn't she see he wasn't good enough for her? There had to be men out there who'd love her as she should be loved. Who'd never hurt her, never let her down as he had. His hand tightened on the steering wheel as he headed down the road, away from her little house as fast as possible. Away from the temptation to go back to her and promise he'd never, ever let her down again if she'd give him just one more chance. But he had to be strong and put himself second. He loved her with every fibre of his being, and then some. But she deserved a better man than him.

She loves me.

He was sorry about that. It wasn't going to do her any good. But she'd get over him and find someone else. He couldn't be trusted to have her back, to protect her heart over everything that might break it, including himself.

In the apartment block underground parking area, he braked abruptly, pushed out and slammed the door in frustration. He'd found Chloe again. Found love again. Screwed it all up spectacularly again.

What was wrong with him?

His phone rang. 'Chloe' showed on the screen. He ignored her, shoved the phone into his pocket and headed for the road and the beach beyond.

The phone rang again. 'Chloe.' The phone went back into his pocket.

Storming down the beach, dodging kids and dogs and couples strolling hand in hand, he aimed for the far end.

The next time the phone went he was tempted to hurl it into the sea, but managed to refrain.

Perhaps he should answer, explain to Chloe that he wasn't good enough for her. But hadn't he avoided her last time and been wrong to do so? Yes, he had. But he had to sort his head out before he said something that might cause more repercussions for Chloe. She'd had more than her share of heartache because of him. Chloe came first. Not him ever again.

But this time it was his mother calling.

Good. Now was his opportunity to finally say his piece, to let her know that by saying Chloe was having an affair behind his back she'd gone and broken his heart completely. His finger hovered over the icon.

I'm more guilty for believing her. It was all my fault I didn't listen to Chloe. Not Mum's. Or anyone else's. I really don't deserve another chance with her.

He put the phone on silent and dropped it back into his pocket, continued striding along the wet sand as though an infuriated bull were behind him.

'So that's the way he wants to play it,' Chloe muttered and dropped her phone back on the bench. No surprise. She'd give him some time and try again. Because she wasn't giving up. Been there, done that, and look where she'd landed. On her own and still in love with Dev.

No, this time she would push every button he had to get his attention. They *would* talk about this and if he still wanted to walk away afterwards, then so be it.

Making another mug of tea, she leaned against the bench where only a short while ago Devlin's tight butt had been resting. She sipped the hot liquid and shoved away the urge to cry. Crying achieved nothing except puffy eyes and a headache.

Damn you, Devlin Walsh. You have the power to hurt me so much. Why can't you just stop and talk to me? Listen to me? Tell me what you're thinking. How you feel. What you want.

She'd give him some space to get his head around the fact she'd been pregnant with their baby, and hope he saw the light, and realised there was no point holding onto the past. They'd both moved on. That had been pretty apparent over the past couple of weeks. And making love with him this week had shown how much they were still so in tune with each other. They belonged together. They were two halves of a whole.

No matter what, he wasn't getting away with a repeat of last time. They would talk, and make up, and get on with living the life they'd once dreamt of having together.

Her phone rang.

Her heart lifted.

That hadn't taken long.

But it was Jaz's name on the screen. Ignore her? To hell with that. 'Hey, what's up?'

'What time are you heading into town?'

Eek. She'd forgotten the birthday lunch for their pal, Mackenzie. She couldn't go. What if Devlin tried to get hold of her when she was out with her friends? He'd think she didn't care. But if she sat here waiting for him to call she'd get into a funk. 'The table's booked for one and Mackenzie wanted to go for a drink at the Harbour View first, so how about we meet there at midday?'

'Perfect. I've got the handbag, by the way, and it's gorgeous,' Jaz said.

The present they were giving their friend. 'Thanks for doing that. See you soon.' Chloe stared out of her front windows, willing Devlin to come walking through her front door.

I'm missing you already.

Thunk. Genie head-butted against her thigh.

'Walkie time, huh?' Might as well, since Genie would be alone for a while this afternoon. And who knew? They might bump into Devlin walking on the beach. Except if he was avoiding her phone calls there was no chance he'd be on the beach he knew she frequented.

'How am I going to find the strength to wait him out, Genie?'

Thunk.

'Fair enough. One walk at a time.' But how long did she give him before banging down his door and demanding he talk with her?

Once back inside his apartment two hours later, Devlin finally checked the messages on his phone. He couldn't go on hiding from everyone for ever. What if he was needed in the ED? That would take his mind off everything for a while. The walk had done nothing to calm the turmoil in his head and heart. He loved Chloe. Which was why he had to stay away. He couldn't risk hurting her any more.

'Urgent.' His mother.

'Please call me.' Chloe.

'Got an hour to catch up for a drink?' Mark. His mate from Auckland was in town with his wife to see an art show.

Who to answer? Who to ignore? Damn but it was like juggling melons and knowing there was going to be a mess when he missed the lot. His sigh was harsh. 'Urgent.' Everything was urgent with his mother, but at the moment she would be the easiest to deal with, because he would simply say no to going up to Auckland for whatever dinner or function she had in mind today.

'Mum, what's up?'

'It's your father. He's had a heart attack and is having surgery late this afternoon.' She sounded oddly fragile and his heart missed a beat.

'Surgery for what?'

'Stents. Why aren't they doing it now? He could have another attack before then.'

'No, Mum. That's unlikely. The medical team will be watching him like a hawk.' Hell, Dad, you'd better hang in there, and get through this one. 'I'll be there as soon as possible.'

'Of course you will. I'll let you go so you can arrange a flight.' Just like that, she hung up on him. She knew he'd do what was right.

What she wouldn't understand was that he'd do it because he loved his father despite the difficulties they'd faced over how he wanted to take a step back from the family commitments. He wasn't going up to be by his bedside to please either of his parents. This was about love, pure and simple.

Sorry, Chloe, we'll have to talk later.

When Devlin walked into Auckland General's ICU nearly three hours later he still hadn't called her or left her a message. It didn't sit well, but what to say? He didn't want her rushing to his side because of his father's medical event. When he next saw her it would be because he was ready to discuss their future.

The sight of his father looking so small and frail in bed shocked him. 'Hey, Dad.' A lump filled his throat and he couldn't say any more.

Carefully avoiding all the tubes attached to him, Devlin gave him a gentle hug. And shook his head. 'What are you doing trying to scare us?'

'Scared me, too,' his father gasped.

'You won't know yourself once those stents are in.' Three, according to the cardiologist he'd just spoken to. 'You'll be running round the golf course soon, and won't even need the buggy.' He was a doctor, and he hadn't noticed anything wrong with his father's health.

He got a weak smile for a reply.

'They're taking you down to Theatre in a few minutes. I'll sit with you until the orderly comes for you.'

'Th-thanks, son.'

Devlin stretched his legs in front of him and watched the shallow rise and fall of his father's chest. A strong, forceful man, dropped to his knees by his own heart. A man who never paused to listen to other people's opinions or needs lay there looking lost and a little frightened. That was natural. Devlin had seen it often with patients. Yet it was hard to get his head around the fact his dad could be the same. Not when his word had always been law, his way the only way.

That's not what you're doing to Chloe, by any chance?

No, he was protecting Chloe from himself, by not screwing with her life any more.

You sure about that?

No. Not at all.

An orderly appeared around the end of the bed. 'Right, Mr Walsh, let's get you down to Theatre.'

Devlin gripped his father's hand for a moment. 'See you in a while, Dad.' He watched him being wheeled away and then went to join his mother while she waited for the surgery to be over.

At first neither of them said much, lost in their own thoughts. Devlin kept fidgeting with his phone, wanting to call Chloe and tell her what was going on. He'd give almost anything to have her with him right now. But he couldn't do that. It would be selfish. He'd walked away from her again, so he couldn't ask anything of her. He owed her that much at least.

'Your father's strong. He'll get through this,' his mother said with her usual determination.

Was that how she'd always approached life?

It was the only way he and Patrick had known her. A force to be reckoned with. Someone who'd always wanted things done her way, and that way had to fit in with their father's world. 'Why did you lie to me about Chloe having an affair, Mum?'

'To get rid of her.' No lies, no gentle cover-up. Just the blatant truth.

He'd more than suspected it, but it still hurt to have it confirmed. 'What about me? My feelings for her?'

She took her time, surprising him. Finally she told him, 'Chloe was busy dragging herself out of poverty and nothing would stop her from reaching for a better life. But she wanted to focus on her career; she wasn't really prepared to devote her whole life to you and to the family. She was all wrong for you. I didn't want you being hurt.'

'Your lies hurt me.'

'Chloe would have hurt you more. I saw her out with that man more than once. It was only a matter of time before she betrayed you. Best she went before she made a mockery out of your relationship.'

His anger was rising, but he held it in check enough to say, 'You didn't know Chloe. You only saw what you wanted, and were convinced she didn't fit into your expectations of what my wife should be like. Yet she tried. Oh, man, how she tried.' He stood up and paced to the window and back, stared down at this woman who'd raised him and watched him get his heart thoroughly broken. 'Chloe is the most unselfish woman I've ever had the good fortune to fall in love with. I didn't deserve her.'

'You don't mean that. It's been a long time since you broke up. You should be thinking about settling down now and having children to continue the family name.'

'Mum, stop it.' The words exploded from his broken heart. 'You have no idea what you're talking about.' Back at the window, he stared out onto the busy street below, not really seeing anything but the face he'd loved for years. The endearing smile and cheeky grin, the twinkling eyes that had sometimes filled with tears or love or shock. Shocked betrayal was the last vision he'd had of Chloe as he'd left her that morning.

Was he the same as his mother? Intent on getting what he wanted from people and not really giving enough back? If that was the case, then he didn't have to stay like that. He could change. Would change. If Chloe would give him a second—no, a *third* chance.

Turning, he crossed to sit beside the woman who'd raised him to her exacting standards.

'Chloe is strong and determined to be herself, but she also gives so much of herself to others. She is not, and never was, out to tie herself to someone else's good fortune. She stands tall and proud.' And has her heart bruised and broken, and yet gets back up to fight another day.

'You're seeing her again.' There wasn't even a hint of pleasure in her voice.

'Yes.' At least, he had been. Who knew what his chances of reconciliation were? No, he really didn't deserve to be given another chance. But she had phoned and left messages to call him back. That wouldn't be so she could just vent her spleen. He would crawl over broken glass to win her back. 'I'll stay until Dad's out of Recovery and I've talked to the surgeon, then I'm going home. To Wellington,' he added, in case his mother still believed she ruled him.

'You can't do that.'

'I can and I will,' Devlin said firmly. 'It's for the best, Mum. For all of us. It's not that I don't care about the family. I do. It's that I have my own life to live.' Hopefully he wasn't too late for Chloe to be a part of that.

'He's either not home, or he's ignoring the intercom,' Chloe told Genie as they stood outside Devlin's apartment block the next morning. 'Might as well go home for breakfast.' Not that she felt in the slightest bit hungry, but she'd go through the motions.

It had been a long, sleepless night after she'd got home from the birthday celebrations that had gone on and on. She'd felt guilty for not being full of life during lunch with her friends. When she'd finally managed to sneak away and grab a taxi home, she'd been ever hopeful that Devlin would be sitting in his car outside her gate, waiting to tell her he was sorry for disappearing and that he'd never do that to her again.

Once again she'd been living in la-la land. There'd been no car, no Devlin, no apology.

'Come on, girl.' She tugged the lead, and they began walking home, stopping in at the supermarket for some crumpets in the pathetic hope she might feel like eating when she got home.

What happened to being strong? Twenty-four hours and she was coming apart at the seams. Hadn't she meant it when she said he wasn't getting the better of her this time? That she'd at least try to talk to him and make him see they could make a go of a relationship? Yeah, she had.

Woof, woof. Genie pulled at the lead.

'Hey, steady, girl.' Chloe looked around to see what had got Genie excited, and her heart slammed into her ribs. Devlin, Really? Really. The lead slipped from her lifeless fingers.

He was striding towards her, purposeful and yet visibly worried. 'Chloe.'

'Dev.'

'I tried to get here last night. But it wasn't possible.' Then his arms were around her, finally giving her that hug she'd hoped for during their last conversation. Followed by a kiss. Oh, and what a kiss. It reached to every part of her, loosening the tightness that had held her in a vice-like grip from the moment she'd watched him walk out of her front door and down the path to his car, touching her as only Dev's kisses could. Making her feel whole and real and happy. Happy? She jerked away, locked a fierce look on him. 'Where have you been?'

'Auckland.'

Her arms fell away. The family. Right. 'You couldn't have let me know something, anything, about where you were?'

'Chloe—'

'This reeks of last time. You.' She poked him. 'You refused to talk to me then. What's happened to owning that? You admitted you'd made a mistake and now you're doing the same thing again. No way.' Hadn't he learnt a thing?

'I wanted to be certain of where I stood, what I was going to do. I owe you that much at least.'

'So you went back home to Auckland.' Great. Nothing had changed.

'This is not an excuse, please understand. But Dad had a heart attack yesterday. I flew up, stayed until he came out of surgery and then headed for the airport. Unfortunately there were no seats available on any flights until this morning so I stayed overnight at a hotel at the airport.' He did look remorseful.

But that wasn't enough. 'I'm sorry your father is ill, Dev. But was your phone completely flat? You couldn't even text me to tell me where you'd gone? I've been ringing you, been to your apartment block, even asked if you were at work. Did you think I'd walk away again, let you go without a fight?'

Firm hands gripped her shoulders. 'Look at me, Chloe. I know exactly what I want with you. For us to be together for ever, to have that future we'd once dreamed of. Going to Auckland was out of my control, and I deliberately didn't tell you about Dad because I didn't want you turning up out of sympathy after how our last conversation ended.'

But she would've been supportive and loving—and hopeful. 'Is your father going to be all right?'

'Yes, as long as he's sensible. They put in three stents and when I left he was sitting up in bed demanding to know when he could go home.'

Dev hadn't hung around then. Because their future was more important to him? She had to know. 'You're either all in or you're all out when it comes to us. No half measures, Dev,' she said firmly.

'I am not going back to Auckland for any events or dinners, or any other damned thing my mum comes up with. I'm here, in Wellington, and I've found you again and that's all that matters to me. Nothing is ever going to come between me and you again, Chloe.' He hesitated.

'Go on,' she pushed.

'I don't deserve you but I'm all in. Right over my head.' His hold softened, pulled her a little closer. His eyes gleamed with light and happiness. 'I love you, Chloe Rasmussen. With all my heart and then some.'

Phew. They'd finally done it. Got back on track and were heading towards happiness and an exciting future. She pulled back just enough to be able to lock her eyes on his. 'I love you, Devlin Walsh, and you do deserve me. Nothing else matters.' Very happy. 'Dev, I know there are things to talk about, but I promise you I've never stopped loving you since the day I first met you all those years ago. Will you marry me?'

A smile lifted that amazing mouth. 'Yes, Chloe, I will. I love you with all my heart and don't want to spend any more time without you at my side.' He pulled her close again for another kiss.

Some time later Chloe leaned back once more to look into those superb, sexy eyes. 'Let's do it soon. There's no reason to hang around for months when we've already wasted years. I'd like to get married asap. And to keep it simple.' She wasn't letting him out of her sight, at least until they'd tied the knot.

'You're on. What are you doing next week?'

'Putting in for leave for our honeymoon.' It had all come together just as she'd hoped.

Giuseppe lifted his glass of champagne and tapped the glass. 'Let's drink a toast to Devlin and Chloe Walsh.'

'To Mr and Mrs Walsh,' Lorenzo said gruffly.

Chloe grinned. 'To us.'

Dev laughed. 'To us. And to you all, family and friends, for celebrating this special day with us.'

Eight weeks after her proposal, Chloe was still pinching herself. She and Dev had talked a lot about what had come between them and finally laid everything to rest. How could they not when their love for each other had weathered seven years in purgatory? They'd both changed in that time and were ready to fight for what they wanted. Not that there'd been any fighting. Just lots of laughter and loving and happiness.

Devlin wrapped his arms around her. 'You look beautiful, Chloe love.'

'Oh-oh. Time I brought some food out or these two will become an embarrassment.' Lorenzo laughed.

'I'll give you a hand,' Chloe's mum said.

'I'll help, too,' Ruth Walsh said loudly, always the controller. But at least she and Dev's dad had accepted the wedding was going ahead and it was here, in this small family restaurant with no onlookers, no big society fuss, only family and close friends.

'Of course you can. Giuseppe, what needs doing first?' Lorenzo said.

'Nothing. The mothers are meant to sit down in regal style and enjoy the occasion.'

'Oh, no.' Chloe's mum laughed. 'I can't sit around being useless.'

'And I intend doing something to help.'

Chloe sighed. Ruth had come around to the fact that she was in Devlin's life for ever. It wasn't always going to be easy between them, but Ruth had apologised, albeit stiffly, and they were all trying to move on, and that was good enough for her and for Dev.

Chloe leaned against Devlin, looking around at the people who were here in Giuseppe and Lorenzo's restaurant to share this perfect day with them. 'I have never been so happy.'

'I'll second that,' Devlin said quietly. He tapped his glass against hers. 'To us.'

* * * * *

If you enjoyed this story, check out these other great reads from Sue MacKay

From Best Friends to I Do?
A Single Dad to Rescue Her
Captivated by Her Runaway Doc
The GP's Secret Baby Wish

All available now!